MERCENARY MAGIC

MERCENARY MAGIC

Dragon Born Serafina: Book 1

www.ellasummers.com/mercenary-magic

ISBN 978-1-5169-9669-8

Cover art by Rebecca Frank

MERCENARY MAGIC

Dragon Born Serafina: Book 1

Ella Summers

Books by Ella Summers

Dragon Born Serafina

Dragon Born Alexandria

Sorcery and Science

And more coming soon…

Read more at
www.ellasummers.com

Contents

CHAPTER ONE
Panoramic Battleground

BATTERY SPENCER WAS widely considered the best spot to snap shots of the Golden Gate Bridge. Every day, visitors to the ruins of the former military fort braved bone-chilling wind and fog for a spectacular panoramic view of one of San Francisco's wonders. Today, they were braving the twirling cyclones summoned forth by a psychotic mage with melodramatic tendencies.

Well, perhaps 'braving' wasn't the right word. The crowd stood at the edge of the fort, their cameras pressed against the chain-link fence that separated the ruins from the neighboring plot owned by Magical Research Laboratories. The foolish voyeurs clicked away with insatiable glee, their interest in the bridge temporarily discarded in favor of more exciting entertainment.

Exciting for them. Not for Sera, who didn't exactly consider being slapped against concrete walls fun times. Everyone thought Mayhem, San Francisco's oldest monster cleanup guild, attracted nothing but sadists and adrenaline junkies. In reality, it attracted mercenaries who preferred to eat every day, have working electricity, and keep a roof over their head: all those little delights that came with a steady paycheck. Fortunately—or unfortunately, depending on who you asked—there was no shortage of magical miscreants in the city.

This particular miscreant shot a blast of wind at Sera. She rolled to the side, avoiding it—barely. Her teeth chattered as the arctic gust whipped past her shoulder and jiggled the metal fence. It was never really warm up here at the battery, but this was outright ridiculous. The mage was drawing on the wind, channeling it into his own attacks. Which meant he'd be able to keep going for awhile. Awesome.

"We need to get past those cyclones," Sera told Naomi.

Sera's sometimes-partner looked out across the parking lot of twirling mini-tornados that separated them from the mad mage, her short platinum hair buzzing in the wind. "Yeah. Good idea." There was no humor in her eyes.

Not that Sera could blame her. They'd only been trying to get to the mage for the last quarter of an hour. Now, fifteen minutes might not sound like very long, but it's a freaking eternity when you're locked in battle with a mage who thinks it would be a fine idea to add your blood to the copious layers of graffiti painted onto the ugly green walls behind their captive audience. He'd tried to hurl her and Naomi over the fence more than once—and when that failed, *through* the fence.

The click-happy tourists should have taken that as their hint to run. After all, if that fence fell, they'd be the ones crushed beneath it. But had they run like sensible human beings concerned for their own well-being? No, they'd instead started taking videos. Sera's gravel-pasted denim bottom was probably all over Youtube by now. They even had a special channel on there for all things supernatural.

Yay, fame.

"Try swinging around behind him?" Sera said to Naomi.

"I did try. He's not letting me out of his sight. Apparently, he can toss tornados at both of us at once. I have a feeling he's done this before."

The mage took that moment to hurl a fireball their way. Sera and Naomi split in opposite directions, and the ball hit the fence with a rattle. While Sera was mulling over the fact that the mage could wield *both* wind and fire magic, the spectators had no such sense. A few of them tried to squeeze their hands through the fence to pick up the ball. The fire was out, but the ball was still smoking. They were completely out of their minds.

"Don't touch it!" Sera hissed at them.

They ignored her, as expected. An old man slid his walking stick through an opening in the fence and prodded the smoking ball toward his feet. Sera didn't even know why she bothered.

Mages, fairies, vampires, and all sorts of other magical beasties—the existence of the supernatural was common knowledge. But rather than staying away from magic, people flocked to it. They visited vampire bars. They watched mage duels. And they collected all things remotely magical, even worthless chunks of debris like that spent fireball. They believed that if they could just collect enough magical objects, they themselves would become magical.

Well, it didn't work that way, no matter how much they wanted it to be true. It was a myth spread by the hopeful masses and encouraged along by the Magic Council, the organization that ruled over the entire magical community. They figured that as long as people held out some hope of gaining supernatural powers, they wouldn't go on murderous rampages against them. So far, their plan had worked out pretty well. The Magic Council was smart. They were also complete monsters.

Sera shook the jitters out of her sweaty hands. No one from the Magic Council was here. They were all busy sitting in their marble-floored offices, listening to pretentious mood music while sipping their fancy cappuccinos. And as long as Sera didn't do anything spectacular in front of all those cameras, it would stay that way. As long as they didn't have a clue she existed, she'd be safe.

The mage edged closer to the door he'd been eyeing since Sera and Naomi had arrived on the scene. Whatever was in there, he wanted in. It was their job to make sure he didn't get what he wanted—and to keep the innocent bystanders safe. Sera wasn't sure which of the two tasks was more impossible.

"Get down from there!" she shouted over her shoulder.

A man sat balanced atop the fence, one leg sprawled over each side. He was in his late-twenties, wealthy enough to afford designer jeans and not fuss about ripping them on the fence. He probably had a whole closet of designer clothes. He was handsome—and knew it. As relaxed as a cat lying down for a nap, he lifted his phone over his head and snapped a shot. Then he dipped his chin toward Naomi and gave her a wink. Down below, some of his friends cheered and let out a chorus of catcalls.

"Idiots," Naomi muttered, but the hint of a smile settled on her lips. She just couldn't help herself. It must have been her fairy blood. Fairies loved basking in people's admiration. And people loved admiring them.

Sera returned her attention to the mage. The field of cyclones had settled down somewhat, maybe enough for her to make a run for him. He closed his eyes and rolled back his shoulders, lowering into his knees as he raised his hands in the air.

Uh-oh.

Not only could the mad mage create tornados and toss fire balls, he was a summoner too. The cyclones drew closer to him, as if they were being sucked in. They spun faster and faster, even as they merged into a single spinning wall. It encased him, shielding him as he stood motionless in a summoning pose.

Sera exchanged worried glances with Naomi. She didn't know what the mage was summoning, but chances were it wasn't good. There were many flavors of magic. This mage's flavor was highly destructive elemental magic. It was super unlikely that he summoned cute kittens and bunnies.

"How about you fly in from above?" Sera suggested.

Naomi shook her head. "His cyclone wall is over ten feet tall. I can't fly that high. I'm only half-fairy."

"I'll give you a boost."

Naomi gave her a look that said she'd rather eat gravel. "The last time you gave me a boost, my butt landed in the Pacific Ocean."

That again. That particular mage had turned out to be a short-range teleporter. Like Sera could have predicted that.

"He looks too busy summoning the creature of our destruction to teleport away," Sera said. "And he's not about to abandon that door, not after all the effort he's gone through to get to it. Come on. I'll give you a boost over the wind wall, then you just flutter down beside him and blast him in the face with some Fairy Dust. Easy-peasy. It will be fun."

"Sera, you and I have strikingly different ideas of what constitutes fun." Naomi sighed. "But I don't suppose we have much of a choice anyway."

Naomi backed up as far as she could, which put her back flush against the fence. Fingers poked through the gaps in the chain-link pattern as everyone tried to squeeze in a lucky rub. Naomi didn't flirt with them this time. She burst into a sprint, picking up speed with every stride. She sprang up, kicking off the launch pad Sera had formed with her hands. Sera pushed up to give her that extra boost—then held her breath as Naomi shot toward the wind wall. If she hit it, she'd bounce right off and get hurled clear across the parking lot. And that would be a whole lot worse than landing in the ocean.

Naomi slipped over the lip of the wind wall, narrowly missing it as she rolled upright. She fluttered down gently into the eye of the storm and landed right beside the mage. As she set down, she threw out her hands, blasting him with a shot of Fairy Dust. Sera could just make out the cloud of twinkling gold and silver particles through the windy barrier. The mage swayed to the side, but he did not go down. The storm weakened for a second before blaring up again, stronger than ever.

"Uh, Sera," Naomi called from behind the wind curtain.

Damn. The mage was too strong. As in, really, really strong. Sera had never seen anyone resist a blast of Fairy Dust, especially not a blast to the face. The mage spared Naomi an irked look, then returned to summoning whatever beast he was about to unleash on the world. The wall of wind was growing. It was up to twelve feet now. A band of flames licked the upper rim. Sera could just make out the fiery form of a dragon forming within the barrier. It was only half the height of the wind wall but growing fast. Sera had to do something. And fast. If she waited until the dragon finished forming, a lot of people were going to get hurt.

She backed up to the fence. Their audience didn't try to rub her. They were, however, shooting videos of the slowly coalescing dragon. Sera made a run for the barrier. She'd have to coordinate this just right, or the whole world would witness the magic she'd spent her whole life trying to hide. And then it would only be a matter of time before the Magic Council figured out what she was and sent assassins to kill the 'abomination'.

A fiery tail swept out from the barrier, swinging toward Sera. She hopped aside and drew her sword, swinging the blade down to sever the phantom tail. The barrier shook, and the mage stumbled back. But the effect lasted only a moment. The dragon was made of magic, not flesh. The air sizzled and cracked, stinking of sulfur. A newly regrown tail whipped toward Sera's head. She rolled to avoid a fiery beheading, then slashed out to sever the nasty appendage once again.

A roar of pure fury erupted from the mage's mouth. He'd fallen back to the rear side of the building, which blocked out most of their eager audience's view. Most, but not all. Sera caught a glimpse of Naomi, held in place by a fiery tentacle wrapped around her ankle. The mage was almost done summoning the dragon. And a whole dragon was a hell of a lot worse than a wayward tail. Sera had run out of time.

She darted forward, aiming straight for the stormy barrier. She reached out with her senses, trying to get a feel for its magic. Every type of magic sang a unique tune, a magical musical fingerprint. This barrier sang of arctic winds and scorching fire. It sang of forgotten days and ancient beasts. The song was powerful. It rumbled and roared through Sera's ears. It burned her nose and froze her tongue.

A cool soothing film slid over Sera's skin, invisible but potent. And when she slammed into the barrier, the mage's spells snapped, their magic pouring across her. His eyes wide with shock, it took the mage a moment to lift his hands up once more. It was a moment too long. Sera punched him hard in the head, and he went down, his magic dissolving into thin air. The fire and wind were gone. The dragon too.

"How did you do that?" Naomi asked, kicking off the last lingering remnants of the fiery tentacle.

"There was a hole in the barrier. I snuck through."

Naomi's slender brows lifted, but she said nothing. For that, Sera was grateful. Naomi wasn't just her partner; she was her friend. And Sera didn't like lying to her friends. She would and did—every day of her lie of a life, in fact. She just didn't like it. But it was either lie or risk exposure. If the Magic Council found out about her, she'd be sentenced to death for the crime of being born. They'd kill her sister too. If they happened to be feeling particularly self-righteous that day, they might even kill her brother. So, yes, she was going to keep on lying and living.

Sera swung the dozing mage over her shoulder and followed Naomi around the side of the building. Down below, a blanket of fog rolled out from the city, smothering the bridge in layers of ethereal mist. The excitement finally over, most of their audience had returned to taking photos of the scenic view. A few of them, though, had their cameras aimed at her and Naomi. As Sera dumped the mage in the back seat of Naomi's car, she sighed. Hiding her magic would have been a whole lot simpler in a world without cameras and the internet.

CHAPTER TWO

Magical Might

SERA TRUDGED DOWN the sidewalk toward home. The small house she shared with her sister and brother was in Richmond, the San Francisco district wedged between the Presidio to the north and Golden Gate Park to the south. That put her smack dab in the middle of most of the city's magical chaos.

Ever since her battle with the mage near Battery Spencer, it had been one thing after another. Later that night, it had been drunk vampires starting bar fights all across downtown. Yesterday, it had been two warring herds of centaurs that had decided it would be a swell idea to turn Golden Gate Park into the battleground for their bloody dispute. And today it had been caterpillars. Lots and lots of monstrous, moody, gigantic wolf-sized caterpillars. Sera was bruised, sore, and her boots were pasted with oozing clumps of mucous-colored caterpillar guts.

She just wanted to take a long, hot shower to wash away the grime and soothe her aching muscles. And after that, eat. Tonight was Friday, which meant pizza. Sera loved pizza. It was the perfect remedy to a perfectly horrendous week.

She stepped into her bedroom just long enough to hang up her sword, then headed for the bathroom. As she washed magic caterpillar goo off of her hands, she glanced at the unicorn clock over the bathtub. Riley wouldn't be back from school for another ten minutes, just enough time for her to hop into the shower.

But before she could soothe her aching muscles in hot steam, the front door thumped open, and the sound of voices trickled down the hall. Riley and someone else, a man whose voice she didn't recognize. They were laughing. Sera turned off the sink and headed back to the entryway.

Riley sat on the bench by the door, his back bent over as he took off his shoes. His school backpack lay at his feet, the words 'Department of Magical Sciences' printed across the front pouch. He looked up at her, his green eyes half-amused, half-apologetic. Sera knew that look. It was Riley's guilty look.

"You're early," she told her brother.

"So I am." The look in his eyes persisted.

"Where's the pizza?"

"Well, Sera, it's like this." He stood, his feet shuffling softly across the floor as he walked toward her. "There's this cafe right along the way home from campus. It's supposed to be really good. Or so all the reviews say." His eyes sheepish, he handed her a paper bag. It was still warm. "We got you a gourmet chicken sandwich."

Sera didn't want a stupid gourmet chicken sandwich. She wanted a pizza. A big, cheesy, glorious pizza. She'd been looking forward to it all day, since even before the caterpillar fiasco.

"Who's 'we'?" she asked, checking her tone.

"Kai and I. He's the one who told me about the cafe."

Sera unlocked her jaw and folded her hands together. "And just who is Kai?" Clearly, someone who was a bad element. Only a bad element would have the audacity to mess with pizza night.

"A friend from my running club." He looked over his shoulder. "Come on in, Kai."

A dark-haired man stepped inside, carrying a paper bag in each hand. He wore dark jeans with a hint of silver undertone, and a fitted ink-black t-shirt that hugged the smooth muscles of his chest, leaving nothing to the imagination. He might as well have printed 'I crack walnuts with my biceps' across the front. Riley said he'd met Kai at his running club, but his new friend looked like he'd be more at home lifting weights in the gym than hitting the trails. Though there was a certain suppleness to his movements. Like a fighter. A damn strong fighter who hit hard and didn't miss.

But that wasn't what made Sera's adrenaline pump into overdrive. It was Kai's eyes. They shimmered like blue glass and burned with raw power. Magic, ancient and dangerous, wound across his body, draping him from head to toe. It ignited the air around them, burning Sera's lungs. It snapped and cracked and promised of punishments cruel and painful. This is what it must have felt like to stand before a dragon—a *real* dragon, back when they'd still roamed the earth. Those fiery beasts that mages summoned were mere shadows of the real thing.

Sera looked at Riley. Surely, he felt it. Kai was an aura of magical might. Never before had she met someone so saturated with power.

But her brother gave no indication that he felt anything of the sort. He was giving her an odd sort of look, though.

"Is something wrong, Sera?"

Yes, they needed to get out of there. Now. "No," she said.

"I'm Kai," said the magic lightning rod, amusement dancing across his lip. He extended his hand.

Every instinct in her body was screaming for her to run, to escape the predator Riley had invited into their home. Instead, she took his hand and shook it. A spark shot up her arm—magical, dangerous…and a bit exciting. She dropped his hand and backed up a step.

"Please excuse us for a second, Kai." Her words slushed out as a hurried mush.

She grabbed hold of Riley's hand and pulled him into the kitchen, closing the door behind them. Then she spun around to stare him down.

"What have you done?" she said in a hissed whisper.

Riley leaned against the edge of the small table they'd stuffed into the corner of the kitchen. He pressed his crossed arms to his chest and glared on back at her. "I don't know what you mean. Am I now not allowed to have friends or something?"

"Sure, have all the friends you want. Just not *that* friend."

"You've known him for all of two seconds, and already you're judging him. Is this about the pizza?"

"No."

He gave her a hard look.

"Ok, maybe it's just a little about the pizza. That was really uncool, by the way. You can't just go changing pizza night. Fantasizing about pizza was all that kept me going when I was up to my waist in demonic jumbo caterpillars."

Riley rolled his eyes. "You're being melodramatic."

"Forget the pizza." Sera dropped her voice back to a

whisper. "Your *friend* is dangerous."

"How?"

"His magic."

"Magic?"

"Really? You don't feel it?" She spread her arms. "That pulsing beacon of primeval power."

He snorted. "Have you been reading those naughty books again?"

"Please take this seriously, Riley."

"Sorry." He coughed. "Ok. *Seriously*, Kai doesn't have any magic."

"He does."

"I may not be a magic detector like you are, Sera. But I can sense when someone's magical. Kai is not."

It was as though they were talking about a completely different person. Unless…

"He's masking his aura," she said.

It was the only explanation. Of all the magical beings, only mages could do it—and only a handful of them at that. It took more power and control than most of them had. There was also the pesky little problem that the more magic you had, the more disciplined you needed to be to cover it up. Kai was gushing magic out of his pores. To mask that from everyone, his self-control must have been absolutely mind-boggling. And dangerous. Very, very dangerous.

"Why would he cover it up?" Riley asked. "That doesn't make sense. You're being paranoid. He probably just handled a magic mushroom or winged cat or something at work today."

"What does he do?"

"He's a vet."

Right. Like there was any way a man with *that* body

spent his days patching up wounded animals. Working security maybe. Or wrestling vampires naked. Yeah, she could totally picture that.

A low chuckle drew her out of her own mind. "If you like him that much, I could arrange to be somewhere else tonight."

"Huh?"

"You know, so you could take a closer look at 'that body'."

Dear God, she hadn't actually said that out loud, had she?

"Though I have to admit that I'm kind of grossed out at the thought of you fantasizing about my friend naked."

Oh, yes, she had said it aloud. Sera swallowed hard, her cheeks burning.

"But I suppose it's better than tossing him out. Which is what you're planning on doing, isn't it?"

She took a deep breath. "Do you remember the assassin who came for me and Alex eight years ago?"

All life drained from Riley's face, leaving him pale as a ghost. "Of course, I remember." He cleared his throat. "The bastard killed Dad."

"That assassin was a first tier mage. Not only that, he was the most powerful first tier mage I'd ever met." She shifted her gaze to the closed door. "Until today."

Riley didn't say a thing. He just stared at the door.

"You know I can sense these things. So trust me when I say that no magic mushroom or winged cat could make anyone's magic feel like that. His magic is ancient and powerful, and he's deadly. Most people are not killers. Sure, they may puff out their chests, throw up their arms, and make melodramatic threats to kill random strangers who bump their bar stool. But it's all talk. You can see that when you look into their eyes.

"When I look into Kai's eyes, I see someone who wouldn't hesitate to kill a person he felt deserved it. He's cold and he's calculating. And based on how effectively he's masked his aura, he's very likely the most disciplined person I've ever met. All of that together spells danger—and lots of it. We need to stay well away from him."

Sera angled toward the door. "Stay here. I'll ask him to leave. If we're lucky, he hasn't yet figured out what I am."

What she didn't tell Riley was that she didn't hold out much hope for that possibility. Anyone that powerful would have felt her weird magic instantly, even though she was masking it too. But maybe he didn't care. Or maybe she'd have to fight him. If that turned out to be the case, she preferred to do it without Riley in the room. She was a brutal fighter, and her little brother didn't need to see that.

Sera stepped into the living room, brushing the door shut behind her. Kai stood beside the coffee table, his cool blue eyes holding her gaze, tracking her progress across the room. She was nearly to him when the front door swung open. Proving that every bad day was just waiting to get worse, three vampires flooded inside, their red eyes gleaming with rage.

CHAPTER THREE

Vampires and Dragons

THEY WERE COMMON vampires, not shapeshifters or demon-powered. Thank goodness for small favors. But they didn't need powerful magic to tear her to bits. Vampires—even common ones—were no joke. They moved fast, hit hard, and could take a beating. The vampire elite liked to use these monsters as foot soldiers. They dealt a lot of damage and were completely expendable, at least as far as the vampire elite was concerned.

From the red gleam in these vampires' eyes, they were caught up in blood rage, which meant they'd be even tougher than usual. They lumbered forward, their muscular bodies clashing with their sickly, sallow skin. Glistening threads of beaded saliva dangled from their fangs, and their eyes screamed hunger. Every single one of those eyes was fixed on Sera.

Her sword was in her room, too far away. They'd be on her before she could get to it. She drew the knife strapped to her thigh. It wasn't designed to decapitate, but there was more than one way to kill a vampire.

"Stay in the kitchen, Riley!" she shouted over the

beastly grunts.

She heard the kitchen door slide shut again.

The vampires charged through the apartment, toppling a side table and scattering chairs in their mad rush to get to her. Sera launched the knife. It hit a vampire square in the forehead. He went down so fast that the other two stumbled over his body. Wet snarls rattled their teeth. They came at her, swinging their clawed fists around with skull-shattering force. She ducked, and the vampires smashed each other in the head. Bone crunched. Sera darted past their falling bodies, retrieved her knife, and quickly stabbed them each in the heart, just to be safe.

"That was impressive."

Sera looked at Kai, who was leaning casually against the wall. His body was relaxed, his eyes amused. Just as he'd been for the entire fight. He had all that magic, and he hadn't even lifted a finger to help. Sure, the vampires hadn't been the brightest bunch, their brains overcooked with blood lust. But they were strong enough that she couldn't risk taking a hit from one of them. Not if she wanted to stand up again. She could have died, and he was acting like it was all some big joke. Maybe he'd even sent the vampires. That was just the sort of thing a first tier mage would do for amusement.

She wanted to scream at him, to demand what the hell was the matter with him. She shrugged instead.

"If you thought that was impressive, you should have seen me chop monstrous caterpillars to bits earlier today."

That's right. I'm just a dumb brute with a sword and a lot of knives. I hack and I chop. There's not a shred of magic in that.

Kai's lip twitched. "I'm sorry I missed it." His eyes panned down her legs, the look in them almost indecent. "I was wondering what that stinky goo all over your boots was."

Or he just thought she stank. But she didn't care what he thought. Not even a little.

"Well, now I have vampire blood all over my clothes to go with the stinky goo."

And why did she just say that? *Oh, right. Because I'm a moron. That's why.*

"Indeed." He reached into his pocket and pulled out his buzzing phone. His blue eyes scanned the screen quickly, then he tucked the phone back into his pocket and looked at her. "There's an emergency at the office. I have to go."

"Kitten with a sprained ankle?"

He gave her a grin—a smug, sexy, satisfied grin. "Goodbye, Sera." He turned and walked toward the door, pausing in front of the kitchen on the way out. "Talk to you later, Riley."

Riley stepped into the hall. "You going to the run at the park tomorrow?"

"No, I have something big going on at work this weekend. I'll try to come next week."

Then he put on his shoes and left.

"Am I allowed to come over there now, or will you chew me out again?" Riley asked when they were alone again.

"I didn't chew you out." Sera grabbed one of the vampire corpses by the shoulders and dragged him toward the front door. "I was trying to protect you." She waved for Riley to follow her back to the living room. "And I can't protect you if you're standing in the middle of the battlefield."

"Maybe you don't need to protect me at all. I'm not completely helpless, you know. I have skills."

"You're studying Magical Sciences. You mix together magic substances in a laboratory."

"Some of them are poisonous. Or explode. Or… Why are you looking at me like that?"

"I was just rethinking your entire education." She pulled her knife out of vampire number two, then swung him over her shoulder. "I'm not sure I want you handling explosives, magical or otherwise."

"Haha."

He lifted the last vampire and carried him down the hall after Sera. Not bad. The brutes were pure muscle and weighed a ton. Riley must have upped his gym hours. Maybe there was a girl he wanted to impress.

Sera nearly laughed. Their life was never that simple. More likely, he'd gotten it into his head to start fighting supernaturals.

"Well, I'm only a few weeks away from graduation," he said. "So it's too late to switch to knitting now."

"Does your school even offer a degree in that?"

"Sure. It's one of the focus points under Physical Manipulation."

"Telekinesis?"

"Yes."

As far as Sera knew, Riley didn't have that sort of magic. He was the best potion maker she'd ever met, but he couldn't summon lightning or hurl fire balls. Or do any magic that would protect him in a fight. And that made him vulnerable.

"On second thought, just stick with the Magical Sciences folks. Those telekinetics are all sort of nuts," she said.

"I've noticed."

They dumped the two vampires next to their buddy. As

they walked back to the living room, Sera shot Mayhem's disposal department a text message to come pick up the corpses. That was one of the perks of working for them. When you killed a monster, they sent a disposal team within thirty minutes. That didn't save her the hassle of filing the report, but at least she didn't have to start digging ditches in the middle of the night. As any regular viewer of horror flicks knew, digging ditches in the dark never ended well.

"We need to talk about your friend Kai," Sera said as she sat down beside Riley on the sofa.

She picked up the bag he'd brought her and reached inside. Damn. The chicken sandwich had gone cold. She took a bite anyway. Double damn. Cold or not, it was delicious. No, it wasn't just delicious. It was the best sandwich she'd ever had. Admitting that to herself hurt her brain. She did *not* want to enjoy anything that had been Kai the dragon's idea.

"I'm not going to stop hanging out with him just because you think his magic is too strong," Riley told her.

"Not just the magic. The eyes. Remember the murderous eyes!"

"Right. So, I'm not seeing that. He's just a normal guy. Or as normal as any of us can hope to be in this messed up world."

Sera gobbled down the last of her sandwich and licked her fingers clean. Then she looked around for more. There wasn't a crumb to be found. She'd already assaulted every last one of them.

"Riley, there's a reason we stay away from magic users."

"You work for a mercenary guild that cleans up supernatural messes. I'd hardly call that 'staying away'."

"I kill monsters. I don't go barhopping with a fraternity

of mage brothers. And Mayhem thinks I'm human, remember? I've gone to great lengths to keep it that way. Even though that puts me at the bottom of the barrel on the pay scale. It's still more than I'd make waiting tables. Which I'd be absolutely horrible at, by the way."

"Yeah, you're much better at beheading things."

"Precisely." She grinned at him. "We all have to make do with the skills we have. Dad trained Alex and me to fight from the day we could walk. He knew that training was our best chance for survival. And he died to ensure that survival. Alex and I are what he made us to be: vicious killers. It's all we know how to do. It's probably all that we'll ever do. But not you. You can be something else. We sent you to school so you could be more."

So far, the three of them had scraped by all right. Her and Alex's pay was enough to live on and to pay for Riley's tuition. Riley was so smart that he could have gotten a scholarship, but they couldn't risk exposure. All scholarships to magical universities went past the Magic Council. They were always on the lookout for magical talent they could later recruit.

In Riley's case, they would have found a non-combative mage with a sharp mind and exceptional potion-making skills, just the sort of talent Magic Council members liked to hire into their own private research laboratories. As soon as they dug a bit deeper, though, they'd have found a family history rife with magical secrets. And the one thing the Magic Council would not stand for was a magical secret. They had to know everything. And they had ways of getting to the truth.

"I know. And I do appreciate what you and Alex have done for me," he said. "By the way, have you heard from her lately?"

Mayhem had sent Alex to Europe on special assignment for some VIP client. She'd been gone for weeks, hunting supernatural baddies. Sera was happy for her—but also sort of jealous. Mayhem had never sent *her* anywhere on special assignment, and she'd never met any VIPs.

"No. I was planning on calling her this weekend," she told Riley. "I don't have to work on Sunday, so I'll probably do it then."

"I hope she's all right."

"Of course she is. She fights even meaner than I do."

He chuckled. "She says you're the mean one."

"Yeah, well, we never could agree on that one." Sera eyed the paper bag on the coffee table, the one with Kai's sandwich inside. "But what we could always agree on was the need to keep you safe. And that's why we need to be very, very careful about the people we associate with. The last time someone found out about Alex and me, Dad died. I don't want you to be next."

"Kai is not an assassin."

No, he's just a mage-eating dragon. But his sandwich sure looked inviting. "I didn't say that he is. I only said that he's dangerous. Which is true. Just look at what happened here tonight. Five minutes after he arrived, vampires attacked us. When was the last time that happened?"

"Sera—"

"Oh, right. *Never.* Because I keep a low profile and don't invite random strangers into our home."

"Kai is not a random stranger."

"Ok, then. What's his last name?"

Riley stared at her for a moment, then blinked. "It never came up."

"I'm not trying to get on your case. I'm just reminding you to be careful. I know it's easy to forget. This is the longest we've ever stayed in one place. After awhile, you stop remembering to always look over your shoulder. You forget that the threat is still out there, just waiting for us to screw up."

"This is no way to live."

"It's the *only* way to live. The other way means death."

Sera grabbed the sandwich bag. It wasn't like Kai was going to come back for it. And if he did, she'd defend her property. Finders keepers.

"For someone who was pretty pissed off about the pizza just a few minutes ago, you sure are devouring those sandwiches fast," Riley commented, watching her chow down on Kai's sandwich.

It was charbroiled beef, which was exactly what she'd have expected from the dragon. "Killing monsters makes me hungry. I've killed a lot of monsters today." She took another bite. "I'm still pissed about the pizza."

"If I promise to bring back pizza next Friday, will you be nice to Kai?"

She swallowed down the last of the sandwich, then frowned at him. "You haven't been listening."

"I have. I just refuse to accept the isolated, paranoid, crazy life you describe for us. How long do you expect us to live like this, hiding from the world?"

"For as long as my and Alex's 'abominable' magic comes with a death sentence for us and anyone around us. Or the Magic Council is toppled. Whichever comes first."

"The Magic Council has been around for centuries. It's not going anywhere anytime soon," Riley said.

"No, it's not. Which brings me back to the need for discretion."

"You're crazy."

"Yes, I am. Very." She grinned. "And you be sure to

remember that the next time you decide to change the menu on pizza night."

CHAPTER FOUR
Mayhem

SAN FRANCISCO WAS one of the world's biggest supernatural hot spots. And within San Francisco, it was the Presidio where you could find the most magic. Twenty years ago, the United States government had delegated management of the park to the Presidio Magic Trust, an organization made up of people hand-picked by the Magic Council. Today, the Presidio had the densest magical population in the entire city. Mages and fairies and vampires lived in fancy new mansions on secluded plots. The Otherworldly—ghosts, spirits, and phantoms—lingered in the old buildings and batteries, tied down to memories forgotten by all but them. There were company buildings owned by the magical dynasties.

There was also a magic school, the one where Riley studied: the San Francisco University of Magical Arts and Sciences. Its campus sat at the southern end of the Presidio.

And not far from there was Mayhem's headquarters. A three-story house with beige and white brick walls, a shingled roof, and bay windows—from the outside Sera's workplace looked more like an upscale villa than a mercenary guild's office building. Grassy green lawns spread out from the house like velvet carpet, ending at a high metal fence interwoven with thorns and roses. It looked posh and proper, just the sort of thing that made Mayhem's posh and proper clients feel right at home.

The fences and thorns also happened to be super useful for defending against supernatural swarms. Even the roses had a purpose beyond pure esthetics. Their pollen was a sedative. So even if invading hordes tried to scale the fence, they'd pass out before reaching the top.

Inside the house, the reception area was awash with marble, glass, and pretentious potted plants. In one corner sat Fiona, the receptionist, dressed in silk, cashmere, and pearls; after all, nothing said 'old money' like pearls. In the other corner, was a coffee and snack bar stocked with cheesecake, muffins, fresh fruit, and a dozen different sorts of granola. There was also an enormous—and undoubtably expensive—coffee machine with its own operator. His name was Fred, and he was cool.

"Hey, Sera. I heard about the vampires," Fred said as she passed in front of the bar. "Tough break. Do you think some magical meanie you thwarted sicced them on you?"

Like everyone else at Mayhem, Fred thought she was human. That's one reason he talked to her—and snuck her tasty snacks that were meant for the clientele.

"Nah, they were probably just smitten with the caterpillar perfume I was wearing." She took the muffin-shaped napkin bundle he'd handed her with a grin, then tucked it into her jacket.

"Dragon-summoning mages, overgrown caterpillars, warring centaurs, crazy vampires. You just can't catch a break, can you?"

"It's not so bad. It's already—" She peeked at the clock

on the wall. "—nine o'clock, and I haven't gotten into a fight yet today."

"Don't speak too soon," he warned.

"That sounds ominous."

"Cutler is in today."

Cutler was one of the most powerful mages on Mayhem's payroll. Though he was a few years older than Sera, he had the maturity level of the average high schooler. The youngest son of one of the city's oldest and wealthiest magic dynasties, he didn't actually need to work. He did it for kicks. Killing monsters amused him. He was cocky and careless, and if you ended up on a job with him as your partner, you knew you were in for a triple helping of hell. If you managed to survive his recklessness, you'd better hope he did too. Because if he didn't, his family would come for you.

"Cutler hardly ever comes in on a Saturday, and he never wakes up this early, even on a weekday," said Sera.

"Exactly. He must be up to no good."

Fred was convinced that at least half of the magic-grade mercenaries at Mayhem were up to no good at any given time. Sera wasn't sure he was wrong about that.

"I'll keep an eye out for suspicious behavior." She gave him a conspiring wink. "Ok, I need to go hit the gym."

Then she headed for the shaded glass doors at the back of the room. They slid open before her, and she entered the real Mayhem. Unlike the ostentatious reception area, the main part of the house was pretty bare bones. The floor of the corridor was concrete painted over in a thick layer of red paint. The walls were plain white, and from the ceiling hung a row of lights that resembled upside-down flying saucers. Sera followed the hallway to the end, then turned right into the locker rooms.

Five minutes later, she was stretching out on her yoga mat in the empty gym hall. Ten minutes after that, she was beating the crap out of a punching bag. In her mind, it had the dragon's smug face and blue-glass eyes. Bam. Bam. He was a threat to her family, and she had to take him down. Bam. Bam. Wiping the satisfaction off that face was just a bonus. She spun around and kicked the bag hard. It swung back—then just froze midair.

"You are a violent woman, Sera."

She stepped sideways to get a look at the man behind the bag. Not that there was any point. She knew who she'd find there.

Cutler stood beside the suspended punching bag, his arms crossed against his chest. His golden hair was stylishly disheveled, his turquoise eyes twinkling with mischief. He wasn't even looking at the punching bag, as though holding it in place with his mind were no more taxing than breathing. It probably wasn't. Cutler was a first tier mage, and his specialty was telekinesis. He could make forks and spoons waltz together across the dining hall's table—by the dozens—and still hold a normal conversation. He was not lacking in the magic department, something he relished in demonstrating at every available opportunity.

"I was training, Cutler."

"You're always training. Don't you ever do anything else?"

"You have your magic to protect you. My life depends on staying in shape."

"Killing monsters when you don't have any magic is crazy. You know that, right?"

Great, the crazy telekinetic—the guy who started levitating everything in sight whenever he got bored—was calling her crazy.

"Thanks for the assessment," she said.

"I like crazy." He stepped forward. "Crazy is fun. Crazy is exciting."

Sera had the sinking suspicion that he was hitting on her. That was disturbing.

"Why are you here, Cutler?"

He stopped, confusion washing his mischievous grin away. "What?"

"It's Saturday. It's not even ten in the morning. And you're here. At work. Why?"

"I came to see you." The grin returned with a vengeance. "There's a party tonight at Liquid. I want you to come with me."

Liquid was the club where the spoiled sons and daughters of San Francisco's elite magic dynasties hung out. It was stuffed full of people just like Cutler. Sera would be about as welcome there as a vampire was at a fairy slumber party.

"Liquid is not really my scene," she said.

"Don't be a tease." As he started walking toward her again, jump ropes, barbells, and weights rose into the air behind him.

"I don't tease. I tell it how it is. And Liquid would spit me out into the street if I ever presumed to enter."

"Not if you're with me."

He gave her a long, assessing look. She was wearing a cranberry-red sport tank and black capris. Her clothes were skin-tight, something he hadn't failed to notice. A flirtatious grin twitched across his lips.

"You have an amazing body, Sera."

"It's the constant training you were complaining so much about." It had shaped her body into a lean and muscular killing machine.

"Then I take it back." He stroked his hand down her ponytail. "Training is good. In fact, we should train together. Vigorously."

He said 'train', but he meant…

"Just imagine the possibilities. With my magic and your body, our passion could ignite volcanos."

Um. Yeah, just um. There were no words—at least none that she could think of. Did those ridiculous lines actually work on other women? Did they lose their minds and throw themselves at him?

"What do you say, Sera?"

That you're really super creepy.

"Care to live a little?"

Sera was thinking up a cordial way to tell him to hit the road, when Naomi stepped into the gym and saved the day.

"Simmons wants to see us right away," she said.

"Ok." Sera looked at Cutler. "I guess we'll just have to finish our chat later." *Like when I have my sword on me. Or at the very least, a taser.*

"Sure thing, gorgeous," he replied with a wink, then swept past her and left the gym hall.

"What was that all about?" Naomi asked as the hovering objects dropped to the floor.

"You really don't want to know."

CHAPTER FIVE

A New Client

NAOMI DIDN'T SAY a word as they climbed the stairs to Simmons's office. She did, however, snicker a few times. After the fifth time, Sera stopped and turned to her.

"Ok, what is it?"

"Cutler is smitten with you." Naomi cleared her throat. "Do you want to talk about it?"

"He's as fickle as a twelve-eyed cat in heat. He'll find a new object of affection before the day is up. There's no point in trying to come up with solutions to problems that will fix themselves."

Naomi nodded. "A practical attitude as always, Sera."

"And if that fails, I'll just knock him upside the head. That tends to clear most men of their ill-conceived notions."

"You certainly have a unique way of dealing with men." A spark of magic twinkled in her aquamarine eyes. "But you might want to think twice before striking Cutler."

"Because of his family?"

"Because he'd probably like it," Naomi said seriously.

Sera had a feeling she might be right about that.

Unfortunately. Well, she'd decimate that bridge when she came to it. She started walking down the hallway again.

"Did Simmons say what he wants?"

Naomi shook her head, and her hair feathered across the tops of her shoulders. Today, it was bubblegum-pink and glistening with silver sparkles. Most fairies had the power to transform their appearance, and some half-fairies did too, at least to some degree. Naomi could change her hair and eye color. Lately, she'd been putting in a lot of hours toward morphing her face, but so far she'd only managed to make her skin turn slightly blue. Of all the magical abilities, glamouring was one of the trickiest. It was more about subtlety and precision than about raw brute force.

"Maybe he wants to shower us with praise for a job well done," Naomi guessed.

"The only way that would happen is if a demon possessed his body and forced him to be nice to us as part of some grand, sinister plan, probably something that involves the consumption of copious amounts of magic mushrooms and dancing naked under the moonlight."

Naomi blinked. "I often get the feeling that you're keeping your best stories to yourself."

Sera grinned back.

A smile cracked her friend's lips. "What do I have to do to hear some of these crazy tales?"

"I only share when under the influence of pizza."

"I'll remember that."

Sera raised her hand to the closed door and knocked. A moment later, a gruff voice beckoned them to enter.

The director of Mayhem had spent decades building the company up from nothing. Yes, he worked hard, but the organization's success could be boiled down to two things:

his knack for discovering talent and his ability to persuade them to come work for him.

The majority of the talent pool was made up of monster-fighting mercenaries. He called them the Street Team. They killed well, but most of them weren't exactly genteel. Simmons knew to keep them and their crude mouths in the field and far, far away from Mayhem's upscale clientele.

For dealing with their paying customers, he had the House Team. They wore silk and pearls, not leather and steel. They were polished and polite. They would never, ever consider punching some snooty old mage lady with a purse full of purple poodle in the face—no matter how much she talked down to them. The old lady, not the poodle. Poodles didn't usually talk, not even the purple ones.

"Sera. Naomi. Please sit down," Simmons said as they entered his office.

Giving Sera a worried look, Naomi brushed the door shut behind them, then quickly walked across the room to sit down on one of the chairs in front of Simmons's desk. Sera followed, her pace slower, her eyes scanning their fearless leader's face for any hint of what he wanted. He didn't look annoyed—well, at least not more annoyed than usual.

Simmons had to be at least fifty, but his face was as smooth and fresh as a man half his age. There were a few magical creams you could buy that would do that, but they were really expensive. Not that he had to worry about money; Mayhem was doing better than ever.

His sandy hair was combed back from his face, revealing a wide forehead and a sturdy jaw. He wore black pants and a black vest over a cerulean-blue dress shirt. His tie was a shade lighter than the shirt, just different enough to match, but not blend in completely. On his left wrist, he wore a fancy watch and on his right hand, a fat class ring from one of the country's magic universities.

Sera took the seat beside Naomi, folded her hands in her lap, and looked up calmly at Simmons. Whatever he wanted, it couldn't be *that* bad. She'd been trying extra hard to behave herself lately. Well, at least since that purple poodle lady incident. Which hadn't even been her fault. The crazy old bat had followed her when she went to deal with the army of angry garden gnomes plaguing her estate. She'd almost gotten them both killed, so Sera had told her off for being a moron. The lady hadn't taken that well and neither had Simmons. Ever since then, he'd been really careful not to give her any jobs with hardheaded clients who felt the need to loom over the 'help' while they worked.

Simmons took his seat. "You did an excellent job on Wednesday at Magical Research Laboratories. You contained the mage before he could cause any substantial damage to either the facility or the surrounding areas. And no one was hurt. Very clean work."

Naomi cupped her hand to her cheek, masking most of her face from Simmons. She arched her eyebrows and mouthed, "Demon possession?" sideways at Sera.

Sera kept her face neutral and her gaze fixed on Simmons.

"The mage who went mad was returned unharmed to Drachenburg Industries, just as our client specified. He's a cousin of the director of the San Francisco office, and they're now all trying to figure out why he went berserk."

Sera had been doing this long enough to know that was code for 'recreational magic drugs gone wrong'. With those filthy rich magic dynasties, it was nearly always drugs. Not that they'd ever admit to it.

"Mr. Drachenburg was very impressed with your work. He's applied a bonus of one thousand dollars to his payment."

That was spare change to someone like Mr. Drachenburg. Someone that high up at Drachenburg Industries probably had at least that much money buried between his sofa cushions. But to Sera, a thousand dollars was a whole lot of money. Too bad Mayhem got to keep most of it. Between their cut and splitting the remainder with Naomi, she might see fifty dollars from it. Fifty dollars was nothing to sneeze at either. She could put it toward a new pair of boots, which was right at the top of her shopping list right now. The caterpillar guts had turned out to have an appetite for leather.

As Sera and Naomi began to stand, Simmons held out his hand. "Sera, stay for a minute."

Naomi gave her a sympathetic pat on the shoulder on her way out. She seemed sure Sera was going to get into trouble for something. But what?

The unruly drunk vampires? They'd trashed three different bars before she even arrived on the scene. As soon as she was there, though, she'd rounded them up pretty quickly.

The centaurs? Their battle had been on a whole other scale compared to the bar fights. But she hadn't been the one in charge. Simmons had sent half of Mayhem's mercenaries and put Zan in charge. She'd done what he told her to do and hadn't even teased him about his silly new hairdo.

Maybe Mayhem's disposal team was grumpy about the pile of caterpillar parts she'd left for them to clean up, and they'd complained to Simmons? But then if they were going to complain, they wouldn't have looked so happy about getting the chance to study a new monster species back in the lab.

Which left the vampires who'd attacked her at home last night. He was going to grill her on them. If only she knew what to tell him.

"Sera," Simmons said after the door closed behind Naomi. He held an open folder in his hand.

"Yes?" she replied, trying not to sound too guilty. She hadn't done anything wrong. She repeated that over and over again to herself in her head until it sounded believable.

"I want you to go to this address."

He pulled a thin strip of paper out of the folder and handed it to her. An address was written on the paper. Somewhere in the Financial District. Maybe where he sent misbehaving mercenaries to get shot. Sera chewed on her lip. Or maybe this wasn't about Mayhem at all. She looked up from the paper and stared Simmons right in the eye. Did he know? Had he figured out what she was, and now he was doing his duty as a good citizen of the supernatural by delivering her to the Magic Council?

"What is it?" Her heart pounded in her ears. Her hands were sticky with sweat. She set them palms-down on her knees.

"The San Francisco branch office of Drachenburg Industries."

Wait, huh?

"Mr. Drachenburg was so pleased with your work, that he wants to hire you for another job. He asked for you personally."

The pounding in her ears faded out. Her fear turned to excitement. No client had ever asked for her by name.

"I've had Fiona clear your schedule. This will be an extended assignment for Drachenburg Industries."

Drachenburg had paid extra to be the only job on her plate for an unspecified time period. Wow. Usually, it was only the veteran mercenaries who got these prestigious jobs. Exclusive paid more—a whole lot more. Maybe she'd make enough to buy Riley a nice graduation present and also a new knife for her collection.

"You're in shock." Simmons appeared amused, which was a new look for him.

"Yes."

"Well, you can absorb it on the way. You have a meeting with Mr. Drachenburg at eleven o'clock to receive your assignment. Don't be late. And whatever you do, watch what you say." He folded his hands together.

"Are you praying?"

"No. Yes." He dropped his hands to his desk, his eyes hard as they met hers. "You're a good fighter, Sera, but you have no brakes on that smart mouth of yours. The Drachenburgs are one of the oldest and most influential magic dynasties in the world. If you screw this up, I'll put you on disposal duty for a month. Understood?"

Sera nodded solemnly. She was good at making messes. She didn't enjoy cleaning them up. "I'll behave myself."

"Good. Now, get over there before Drachenburg fires you on account of your tardiness."

Sera didn't own a car, but she did have a pretty spiffy scooter. Her name was Lily, and she was pink. She was also equipped with a pair of racing wheels and a horn loud enough to give a vampire—or any other supernatural with a case of sensitive hearing—a big, thumping migraine.

Sera parked Lily beside the umbrella rack at Drachenburg Industries, then crossed the vast marble desert that was their lobby. Her sneakers squeaked against the glossy white floor, sliding over the swirly blue dragon at the midpoint of the room. The illustration was stunning, a stroke of whimsical genius in an otherwise cold and dispassionate room.

"Name?" the receptionist said as Sera stopped in front of the desk. The woman's makeup was picture-perfect, as though it had been airbrushed on. Her dark, bouncy curls belonged in a shampoo commercial.

"Serafina Dering."

The receptionist typed a few things into the computer, which then spit out a visitor badge. She slid it across the counter to Sera. "Take the elevator to the 28th floor. You'll find Mr. Drachenburg's office at the end of the hall. Stay on the marked pathways at all times. Drachenburg Industries takes no responsibility for any injuries you may incur—up to and including death—if you stray from the path. Do you understand?"

"Yes."

"Good. Then enjoy your stay and have a pleasant day."

Drachenburg Industries' interests covered all things magical—from potions to poisons, from spells to creatures. They were the world's largest magical research laboratory. Sera didn't know what the San Francisco branch specialized in, but from the receptionist's warning, it must have been something dangerous. Poisonous plants? Experimental sorcery? Fire-breathing tigers?

As long as it's not jumbo caterpillars, she thought and stepped into the elevator. It shot up the chute.

When it reached the top, Sera behaved herself and

followed the path—even though she wouldn't have minded getting a peek at a fire-breathing tiger. Like below in the lobby, the floors here were marble. Paintings hung on the walls, illuminated by spotlight arrays. A few of them bore the distinctive style of Bellatrix Raven, the most famous magic painter in the world.

The blue glass building and everything in it screamed 'money'. No expense had been spared here; in fact, a whole bunch of extra expenses had been lathered on. Standing there, in this hallway that dripped money and magic, Sera felt like she was on a completely different planet. The big magic dynasties didn't see money as an obstacle, or even a tool. To them, money just *was*. They didn't even think about it; it was as natural to them as breathing.

This is why Drachenburg hadn't batted an eye at the hefty premium Mayhem charged for exclusive work. Someone had probably told him Mayhem's mercenaries were the best, and he'd wanted the best. No, he'd wanted *her*. Of all the mercenaries working for Simmons, most of them many times more impressive than Sera on paper, he'd asked for her.

Just don't screw it up.

"Hello, I'm here to see Mr. Drachenburg."

His secretary peered over the computer at her. "Ms. Dering?" Her stare wasn't exactly disapproving; it was more indifferent, as though she'd seen hired help come and go from that office so many times that the novelty of turning her nose up at them had long since worn off.

"Yes."

"Please, go in. Mr. Drachenburg will be with you in a minute." Her gaze returned to the computer screen, and she said nothing more.

Sera walked past the desk and entered the office. A

spectacular view of the bay spread out before her, drawing her across the room with a magic all its own. She'd lived in San Francisco for four years, but she'd never seen the city like this. She stopped before her nose smashed the glass wall and just took a moment to drink it all in. She could get used to that view. And this office.

The room was roughly the size of her house. A desk sat in the corner. Not far from the glass wall, there was a lounge area that consisted of a few leather sofas, two mini-fridges, and three side tables. Atop one sat a picture-perfect basket of fruit. A bowl of chocolates was on the next. And a plate of freshly-baked cookies topped the third. Sera's stomach growled with hunger. Her muffin was still tucked away inside of her locker. She hadn't found the time to eat it yet.

Marble floors. Priceless art. A panoramic bird's eye view of the city. It sure must have been nice to have money. Jewelry. Fancy chocolate. Shoes whose soles weren't peeling off. The possibilities were endless.

The door opened, and the secretary's voice spilled inside. "…Drachenburg, she's waiting for you inside. She's wearing a sword."

"Thank you, Gia."

Sera's brain tried to reconcile that voice with this place. It refused to cooperate. As the door shut with a whisper, she spun around to find him there—Riley's friend Kai, the dragon, the lightning rod of magical might. His blue eyes stared out at her, pulsing with ancient power.

CHAPTER SIX

In the Dragon's Lair

EVERY INSTINCT IN Sera's body was screaming at her to run. This was Drachenburg. The man had seen her fight vampires. Depending on what his mad mage of a cousin had told him, he might even know she'd broken through a wind barrier. Most of all, though, he was strong. Really strong. And the dragon had lured her here, possibly for a midday snack.

Fighting the urge to flee, she bottled up all her magic. Maybe he hadn't felt it yet.

His smile was smooth, his eyes knowing. *Shit.*

She pulled in her magic further, compacting it until it was only a heavy lump in her stomach.

"It's too late for that," he said, his voice deep and rough.

Layer by layer, his power unfolded, like he was shedding a cocoon. It burned and bit, sizzling her in a field of magic. He was testing her. He breathed in deeply, trying to get a fix on her magic. She clenched her jaw and stared him down. He would not crack her.

"What are you?"

Sera didn't answer. Her mind was too busy trying to block him. The thought of attacking him briefly crossed her mind, but she pushed it aside. Simmons would kill her. He'd argue that beheading clients was much worse than telling off purple poodle ladies. Spoilsport.

"Your magic is strong," he said, stepping forward. There was a hint of awe in his voice.

"What magic? I have no magic."

His blue eyes shone out, blinding her in the search scope of his magic. He'd closed most of the distance between them. There was nowhere to run and precious little room to fight. Sera reached down to the knife at her hip.

"Planning on skewering me like you did those vampires?" His brow twitched. He thought this whole thing was all enormously funny. Well, good for him.

"No, I don't skewer mages." Usually.

"Glad to hear it." He folded his arms across his chest. "Tell me about your magic, Sera."

He said it like he fully expected her to answer. Yeah, so not happening. The Drachenburgs were one of the oldest magic dynasties. Duty was tattooed into their sub-conscious. If he figured out what she was, he'd feel compelled to turn her in to the Magic Council. And those distinguished men and women, leaders of the supernatural community, would kill her.

"There's nothing to tell," she said.

"I can feel it." Magic pulsed in his eyes. "You're delusional if you think you can hide that much power."

Well, it had pretty much always worked before. "Look, whatever you think you're feeling, you're wrong," she said. "Just think of me like a magic mushroom."

"A magic…mushroom?" Sera couldn't tell if he was

bewildered or amused.

"Right. Magic mushrooms have magic in them, but they don't *use* magic."

All emotion—bewilderment, amusement, or otherwise—wiped from his face. He gave her a hard look. "You don't feel like a mushroom."

She said nothing.

"Fine, keep your secrets." The hard lines of his mouth melted into a satisfied smile. "I'll find out eventually."

Over my dead body. Which, come to think of it, was exactly how this would all end. "What do you want?"

The dragon's grin widened. *Oh, yes,* it said, *I'm going to eat you for dinner, but I'll save your bones to munch on for a midnight snack. I might even toast them first.*

"Why did you hire me?" she clarified.

In an instant, the dragon disappeared, and his expression shifted gears to the professional, civilized businessman he pretended to be. "Do you remember what happened at Magical Research Laboratories?"

"Sure." It was sort of hard to forget a crazy mage who summoned dragons and wielded the power of tornados and firestorms. They weren't exactly a dime a dozen. "Your cousin went berserk."

"Spontaneously berserk. Without warning."

Hmm. So the hallucinations spawned by smoking magic weeds weren't warning enough?

"I know what you're thinking."

No, you don't.

"And Finn wasn't taking any drugs when he went mad."

"You're a telepath?"

"No."

"Good."

"But everyone always assumes drugs." He held her gaze,

amusement woven into those intense eyes. "The thought of me inside of your head scares you. Is there something in particular you're afraid I'd find there?"

"Dead bodies."

His gaze flicked to her sword. "That I can believe."

"Ok." Sera stepped away from the window and circled past the desk. He was too close. "Is your cousin back to normal now?"

"Yes, he woke up shortly after you dropped him off with my crew. He was back to himself again. How did you do that?"

"I hit hard."

He laughed. The laugh rumbled in his chest, buzzing beneath the black t-shirt he wore. His shirt looked exactly like the one he'd worn last night—or at least its twin brother. So did the jeans. He probably had a whole closet full of that same badass outfit.

"You're staring." The smug bastard was smiling. "Like what you see, do you?"

She hoped he choked on his own narcissism. "You're not wearing a suit."

"Pardon?"

"You're a businessman. Businessmen wear fancy suits."

"Not all."

She ignored him. "They don't dress like they're ready to visit a supernatural biker bar."

"I don't like suits. They aren't comfortable."

"You own this glass castle monstrosity. I'm sure you can afford a custom-made suit. Hell, I bet you have Armani on speed dial."

The dragon snorted. Luckily, fire didn't shoot out of his nose. "Do you always have such a smart mouth?"

"Yes."

"Mayhem's clientele consists mainly of arrogant, stuffy mages from aristocratic magic dynasties."

She arched an eyebrow at him.

"*I* am not stuffy," he said. "However, most of Mayhem's clients are not only stuffy; they are quick to take offense and slow to forgive."

"And?"

"And how do you stay out of trouble?"

"I don't."

"Mr. Simmons assured me that all his mercenaries are exceptionally well-mannered."

This time, it was her turn to snort. Simmons didn't believe that nonsense he was spewing. Not for a second.

"No, I didn't believe him," he said. "And I didn't care. When Simmons realized that he wasn't going to dissuade me from hiring you, he started to sing your praises pretty sweetly."

Aww. Sera would have to remember to send Simmons a muffin. Or at least a bagel. "And why did you insist on hiring me for this job? I'm rude and underpowered. There are dozens of other mercenaries at Mayhem with much better profiles. In fact, *anyone* at Mayhem has a better profile."

"Profiles can be forged. Like the part of yours where it says you don't have any magic."

"Not that again. I told you—"

"Finn remembers what happened during the entire time his magic was going haywire," he cut in. "He couldn't stop whatever force was controlling him, but he remembers everything he did. And everything you did. He saw you shatter that wind barrier."

Her pulse raced, and her heart was making a pretty solid effort at bursting through her chest. All the while, the fear was spreading magic to every corner of her body. She pushed down, forcing it back into hiding.

She cleared her throat. "A force was controlling him, you say? What kind of force?"

"We don't know. But whatever it was, it made him stronger. A lot stronger. Finn is a fourth tier mage. I read your report, and there's no way he could do anything you described. Not even close."

Mages were classified into six tiers, with one being the highest. Those were the most powerful, the ones who were both revered and feared. There were very few first tier mages, and Sera was looking right at one. First tier mages had a personality to match the power. She reminded herself of that.

"How big was the dragon Finn started to summon?" he asked.

"It would have been around fifteen feet long once fully summoned."

"His usual dragon is the size of a cat, not a house."

That certainly was a big difference. The tornados and firestorms weren't a small matter of magic either.

"So, you brought me here for a play-by-play of the incident?" she asked. "Because it's all in my report, you know."

"I saw." He leaned forward, his shoulder brushing against hers as he reached for the folder on his desk.

She jumped a bit, which seemed to amuse him.

He opened the folder and scanned down the top page. "You were very thorough. I found your description of the swaying wind funnels very poetic." He tossed her report back onto the desk. "But that's not why I hired you. You're here because I need you to help me figure out who is behind my cousin's odd behavior."

"You make it sound like a conspiracy."

His icy blue eyes went completely cold. "Last month, another cousin of mine went berserk while on visit to our New York City office. The resulting magical catastrophe destroyed most of a city block."

"I thought that was a bomb."

The footage had made national news. Shattered glass, warped steel, concrete crumbs…a graveyard of dead bodies. Compared to that, Wednesday's fiasco at Magical Research Laboratories had been nothing more than a minor skirmish.

"We covered it up," he admitted. "We couldn't have the general human population getting riled up into a panic. If they knew that mages were going mad and getting a big boost in power, that would be bad for everyone. New York and San Francisco weren't isolated incidents. There have also been break-ins at all our other offices across the world. In fact, San Francisco was the last one to be hit. We knew it was coming, and that's why I came to take over this office for awhile."

"To bite their heads off and breathe dragon fire?"

"Something like that. But we didn't consider that the perpetrator would hit the Sausalito facility. Anything of real magical significance is kept here, not there."

"You think that whoever is responsible for this is trying to steal something from you?"

"Yes. We just don't know what. All those break-ins at all those different offices—yet nothing was stolen. Not the centuries-old magic blizzard staff. Not the fire diamond necklace. Not the summoning tiara. Whoever is hitting us, they're looking for something very specific. And they've figured out how to bypass our facilities' security measures."

"What kind of security measures are we talking about?"

"Poisonous firefly swarms. Modulating elemental cannons. Hallucinogenic fog."

In other words, the best security an abundance of money and magic could buy.

"I see two possibilities," she said. "One, we're talking about a very powerful mage or group of mages."

He shook his head. "I designed our security. No one could break through it. I don't care how powerful he—" He dipped his chin to her. "—or she is."

"Nothing is foolproof."

"My system is."

Right. Ok, then. "That leaves option number two: it was an inside job."

His whole body went rigid. He looked like he could have chewed rocks with that jaw. "The only ones with the necessary access to bypass the security are my own family. I coded their magic into the system—and only their magic. They can turn off the security system by performing a secret sequence of spells. Even if someone else knew the spells, they couldn't get through."

"It sounds like you really thought this through."

"Of course."

"How many people in your family did you code into the system?"

"Twenty-two."

"Didn't anyone ever tell you that the more people know about a secret, the harder it is to keep?" At twenty-two people, it was pretty much impossible. As far as security holes went, this one was crater-sized.

"None of them betrayed us."

Family loyalty was one thing, but this was just plain old thickheaded denial.

"I had a triad of first tier telepaths put a lock on every

single one of us. We're unable to bypass the traps for any other reason than to uphold our family interests. The spell kills anyone who tries to bypass the security for selfish or nefarious reasons."

Forget that. This wasn't denial. It was paranoia of dragon-sized proportions.

"There's something else," he said.

"Oh?" Could it get any worse?

"It's the thieves. Each time, after scavenging around the vault, they simply vanished into thin air."

"What does the security footage show?"

"They disabled the feed."

"Every time?"

"Yes."

"What about the guards? Did they see anything?" she asked.

"People in black with masks. But the guards never got very close. The thieves always set up a barricade, and a few mages defended their position to give the others time to look through the vault. They liked to set the guards' hair on fire."

Sera would have cringed to say that. The dragon didn't even blink.

"At some point, the mages stopped setting off firecrackers, and the guards moved in. The intruders were gone."

"Odd."

"Yes," he agreed. "Who is this group? What are they looking for? Why do they want this object? How are they able to get into our vaults, and how do they always escape?"

"It sounds like you've got a fine mystery on your hands."

"We." His voice was sharp, the single syllable infused

with his will and magic.

"Sorry?"

"*We* have a fine mystery on our hands. You and I. I hired you, remember?"

"You hired the wrong person. What you need is a private investigator. I'm a dumb brute armed with steel. I hack monsters apart with my sword."

"After the conversation we've just had, you honestly expect me to believe you're just a dumb brute?"

Sera folded her hands together and gave him a simple, unassuming smile. "Yes."

Something rumbled in his chest, either laughter or fire. "Come on. Let's go. And bring that sword. I have a feeling you'll need to do a fair amount of hacking before this is all over."

What girl could resist a romantic offer like that? "No."

"No?"

"No. N-O. It might be an unfamiliar word to you, so look it up. It comes after M—and right before I go get my sword."

"Funny."

"I don't want to work with you. I don't trust you."

"Why not?" He looked genuinely surprised.

"Because you pretended to be my brother's friend," she said. "Why would you even do something like that? What the hell is the matter with you?"

"I wanted to get a good look at you before I hired you. Finn's story of what you did sounded too spectacular to be true. I had to see it for myself." His voice was dispassionate, his eyes calculating. He was watching her closely, waiting for her to give something away.

"See for yourself? You mean, by sending a bunch of vampires to attack me in my home?" she demanded.

"No, I didn't send them." He didn't frown, but his eyes had taken on a harder glint. "With your power level, you must be attracting all sorts of weird creatures all the time. Like a magic beacon."

Hmm.

"It happens to anyone with significant magic. The more powerful you are, the worse it is."

Sera had never heard that.

"Even if you manage to mask it, you can't do that all the time. Sometimes, that wall cracks when you sleep. Sometimes when you're hurt. Or tired. Or distracted." He smiled. "You get the idea. When the wall weakens, that's when the monsters find you, drawn in by the taste of your magic. Some mages can sense magic just like the monsters."

That Sera did know. Because she was one of those mages. She experienced magic like it was just another sense —and yet it used all the other senses. She tasted magic. She heard it. She saw and smelled and touched it. All of it and all at once.

"Unlike the monsters, though, I don't just sense where magic is. I identify the kind of magic," he said. "I wanted to get close to you so I could figure out what kind of magic can do what Finn described."

This was going downhill fast.

"But for the first time ever, I couldn't define someone's magic. I've never before felt anything like yours. It's exotic." He inhaled, drinking in the magic in the air, that magic she was trying so desperately to bury down deep inside of her. "Enticing. Delicious. I could drink in your magic all day. You're not mundane, no matter what you pretend. I'd love to fight you to see what you can do. I've only caught a glimpse, but I bet you're even more spectacular than I imagine."

She felt his magic reach out, a tentacle of invisible power wrapping itself around her. It rippled in warm waves against her back, trying to knead the magic out of her. The caress was gentle, even intimate. And it felt like bathing in a hot rose oil bath. She knew he was testing her, hoping that she would use magic to block him out. It felt so good that she almost didn't care.

But she had to care. She had to keep this secret—and not just for her. For Alex and Riley too.

She pushed out her best glower. "You're arrogant," she told him. "You use people to get what you want. Except you don't even see them as people. You treat them like they're tools or—worse yet—toys to play with. You manipulated Riley into thinking you were his friend, just to satisfy your curiosity about me. That's cold and it's mean. And you're not even a very good liar. No one would ever believe that a cruel, arrogant sociopath could be a vet. You actually have to be a real person to care about animals."

He shrugged. "Our labs do a lot of research on magical creatures. And I do like dragons."

Why am I not surprised? "Dragons eat other animals. And people."

He gave her a long, lethal grin. "Come on." He waved his hand toward the door. "We have to get going."

"I didn't say I was going to work with you."

"No, you didn't. You were too busy establishing what a tough and rough fighter you are. You've had your fun, and now it's over." He pulled a bundle of papers out of his desk drawer. "Here's my contract with Mayhem. It says here that you will be working for me until my problem with the thieves is resolved. Do you really want to break the contract?"

Sera didn't, and she suspected he knew that. If she were

the one to break Mayhem's contract with Drachenburg Industries, there would be consequences. One of them was financial, but that wasn't even the worst of it. More than the money, she was worried about the questions. There'd be a lot of them. Simmons took his contracts very seriously, and he'd apply enormous pressure on her to figure out why she'd had the nerve to break one. He'd shove her into the spotlight, where there was a very real danger that her secret could be exposed.

So she followed the dragon out, knowing that her doom might already be sealed either way.

CHAPTER SEVEN

Underpowered

THEIR FIRST STOP was just down the hall. The dragon led her into an office that while smaller than his, was no less extravagant. Floor-to-ceiling wood bookcases packed full with richly colored leather book spines covered an entire wall of the room. The desk, too, was made of wood; a miniature model of an old style San Francisco trolley perched prominently on one corner, a glass jar of colorful bubblegum balls on another. A Wizard House Pizza box was stuffed awkwardly into the trashcan in the corner, the faint scent of cheese and sweet tomatoes lingering in the air. Sera's stomach growled in appreciation.

Finn, the mad mage who'd tried to magic-slap her into oblivion just a few days ago, stared up from the white leather sofa in the corner. He raised his tea cup in meek greeting, looking every bit the part of the underpowered fourth tier mage in a family of magical powerhouses. Not only did he look weak, he felt that way too. He wasn't even a shadow of that mage from Wednesday—not in power level, madness, or confidence. He was through and through a complete pushover.

"Kai," Finn said, standing. His gaze slid slowly over to Sera before dropping to the floor.

"Finn, this is Sera. She's going to ask you some questions. You might remember her as the woman you recently tried to kill."

If Finn's gaze could have sunk any lower, it would have. His shoulders hunched over into a spiritless slouch.

"You're mean," Sera told the dragon, bumping his arm out of the way as she extended her hand to Finn. Anyone who understood the awesomeness that was Wizard House Pizza couldn't be all that bad. "Hello, Finn. I know you've been through a lot, but if you can, I'd like you to go over everything you remember from that day."

The dragon's eyes narrowed. "Why are you being so nice to him? He tried to kill you."

"He didn't mean to."

"So, basically, what you're saying is you'll be nice to me only after I try to kill you—as long as I don't really mean it."

"Yes, exactly that." She flashed her teeth at him. "How about you make your move and see what happens?"

But he was far too smart to be goaded. He locked a stony glare on her. "If I attack first, you can claim self-defense."

"Yes."

"Oh, no." His hard mouth slid into an even harder smile. "You're not getting out of this assignment so easily."

"Should I leave?" Finn asked, his eyes shifting uneasily between them.

His cousin turned to him. "You stay right where you are while Sera asks her questions."

Finn sat back down, folding his hands together on his lap. As Sera sat beside him, he began to fidget with his fingers, twisting and turning them with a nervous twitch. The dragon remained standing, looming over them like a mountain.

"What do you remember?" she prompted Finn.

"Everything," he replied, squeezing his hands together. "Unfortunately."

"You were being controlled?"

He nodded, fear streaking his magic.

"Do you know who was controlling you?"

"No. Only that it was someone very powerful. Or something," he added in a hushed whisper.

"What did this someone want you to steal?"

He shook his head. "I don't know. Something in the vault. I only know I *had* to get to that door. The compulsion was too strong. I couldn't do anything. I was only a passenger along for the ride." He stole a furtive glance at his cousin. "I guess I'd only know what it was I was supposed to be stealing once it was in my hands."

"How were you going to get past the security measures?" she asked.

"I don't know."

"Where did the extra magic you had come from?"

"I don't know."

Well, aren't you helpful. Sera bit back the words. What had happened to Finn wasn't his fault. She wasn't the mean dragon; she could remember that.

"Is there anything else you can tell me that could help us stop whoever is doing this?" she asked.

He paled. "You can't."

"Can't what?"

"Can't stop this. Whoever is doing this is too powerful." He looked at his cousin. "Even more powerful than you, Kai."

The dragon cracked his knuckles. "We'll see about that."

"No. It's too late. Too late for all of us," Finn spluttered out quickly. "I saw San Francisco burning. Legions of monsters tearing through the city. Dead bodies in the streets. Everywhere. The bay bubbled with hot blood. And above it all, high in the sky, a dark, sinister magic hanging over the city like a storm cloud about to burst. The end. The end is coming. A magical apocalypse will crush the city. We are doomed."

"Those were the thoughts of the person controlling you?" she asked.

Finn began to rock back and forth. "The end. The end is coming. A magical apocalypse will crush the city. We are doomed."

"What does the thing you were trying to steal have to do with all of this? Will it bring about this destruction?"

His eyes glazing over, Finn rocked harder. "The end. The end is coming. A magical apocalypse will crush the city. We are doomed."

"Finn?"

"Don't bother," the dragon told her as Finn muttered on. "He's gotten like this every time we've tried to dig too deep. Whoever hijacked his body put safeguards into place."

"This is why we came here. You wanted me to see him like this. Why?"

"I thought it would motivate you to know the city is in danger. From the look in your eyes, I can see that I was right."

Sera stood. Crazy, rambling Finn was too much. The tenor of his magic had changed from nervous to full-out nuts. It was giving her a headache.

"You could just have told me," she said.

"You don't trust me."

He had a point.

"It's better this way," he said. "It's better for you to see for yourself what we're facing. And you won't try to back out of this assignment, not now that you know the stakes."

"You manipulated me." The words scraped against her tongue.

"I'd like to think of it as motivation, not manipulation."

"You can think whatever you want, but that doesn't change what it is," she shot back. "You've done nothing but manipulate me and my brother ever since you poked your head into our lives, and you wonder why I don't trust you. Seriously?"

He stared at her for a few seconds before expelling a martyred sigh. "There are more important things going on here than your bruised ego. You're being hard-headed."

Says the hard-headed dragon.

"Let's worry about saving the city first," he continued. "After that, if you're still mad at me, we can fight it out. I'll even let you throw the first punch. And I won't tell Simmons either."

"Deal," Sera said, grinning.

Oh, he had no idea what he'd just gotten himself into. She'd spent the last twenty years learning how to take down monsters. And when it came down to it, a dragon was nothing more than just another monster.

CHAPTER EIGHT

Replay

A COLD, WET wind bit at Sera's arms and face. If she'd known she'd be paying a visit to the scene of Finn Drachenburg's magical meltdown, she'd have packed her leather jacket. Or at least a sweater. A tank top was no defense against the winds of San Francisco.

Beside her, the dragon looked around the parking lot. His t-shirt wasn't any more wind-resistant than her top, but he walked around like the cold didn't bother him one bit. Maybe he had a fire roaring inside of him—or dragon scales hidden beneath his skin.

"Why are we here? Finn doesn't remember what he was trying to steal. What exactly do you expect to find, Mr. Drachenburg?"

He stopped in front of a wall tie-dyed with black scorch marks, then looked back at her. "Kai."

"Sorry?"

He turned the rest of the way around. "Call me Kai."

"Simmons wouldn't like that very much."

"Forget about Simmons. He's not here. And he's not your client. I am," he said. "I want you to call me Kai."

"Very well. Kai."

It didn't sound as intimidating as Drachenburg. And that was dangerous. Intimidating was good. It reminded her of what he was: a threat hidden beneath a handsome mask.

"Good. Mr. Drachenburg is my father. Or it's what other people—people who revere me, who are scared of me—call me."

"I'm too insubordinate to revere people, no matter who they are. And I'm too stupid to be scared of anyone."

He laughed. "No, you're not. You only pretend to be."

"I hunt down misbehaving monsters for a living. That's not smart; it's pretty damn dumb."

"Dumb and desperate are two entirely different things. You took a dangerous job because you needed the money. The fact that you've survived all these years proves you're not just a dumb brute."

She crossed her arms against her chest. "I am so. You don't know anything about me."

"I know what Riley told me."

"And what was that?"

"That your mother died when you were very young. That you, your twin sister, and he lost your dad when you were only sixteen. You were only a child. You could have run off, but you took care of your brother. You got a job hunting monsters. And because of that money you brought home, Riley was able to get a proper education. That speaks droves about you."

Riley had said too much. He shouldn't have mentioned that she and Alex were twins. Coupled with his suspicions about her strange magic, it might be enough for Kai to put two and two together.

"I haven't seen such devotion to family from most of

the world's esteemed magical dynasties, even though they pride themselves on exactly that."

In his eyes, Sera saw something she'd seen rarely—and certainly never directed at her. Respect. He respected her. It felt...good. It shouldn't have. She shouldn't have cared what he thought of her. He couldn't be trusted.

"You used Riley to spy on me," she said, crunching that reminder into her mind.

"If I was going to hire you, I needed to know what sort of person you are."

He said it as though he didn't even realize what he'd done was wrong. And that was the whole problem. That was why she couldn't trust him. Morality was elastic to him, something that could be wielded as a shield or moved aside when it was too much of an inconvenience.

"I'm a person who doesn't like to be spied on," she told him. "Now, let's get back to why we're here. What exactly do you expect to find here, *Kai*?"

His lower lip twitched. "I'm not sure. Whoever or whatever was controlling Finn was hitching a ride in his body. They might not have been sharing their intentions, but they must have left clues."

"Finn said he couldn't read their mind," she said, chewing on the thought. "But could they read Finn's?"

"You mean, was it more than his body they were using?"

She nodded. "You told me that the only people who could bypass your security are select members of your family. If someone is controlling their bodies and reading their minds, that could be their way in."

"Remember the spell I had put on all of us. Myself included. No one with malicious intent can bypass the security. Based on the apocalyptic slideshow Finn caught, I think it's safe to say this person has nothing but malicious intentions."

"Magic is not foolproof. And this wacko is clearly no ordinary individual."

"True." Kai pulled his phone out of his jeans pocket. His fingers swirled and swiped across the screen. "I'm putting a few more guys on Finn watch. If he starts acting crazy again, we'll know it." He slipped the phone back into his pocket and looked at her. "My people searched this scene right after you brought Finn in. Besides the damage he shouldn't have been able to cause, they didn't find anything out of the ordinary. But I still think someone that powerful had to have left traces, even if he was hiding inside of Finn. Magic of that scale is not invisible. I'd like you to take another look at everything with me now. Go through the motions of the fight, and tell me everything you remember."

"All right."

Sera turned and walked across the parking lot to the spot where she and Naomi had entered the property. She stopped at the gate, then jogged around the cluster of buildings to stand in front of the fence that separated the facility grounds from Battery Spencer.

"When we arrived, Finn had a group of guards caught up in a spinning whirlwind over his head. Over there." She pointed to the building with a large black eight painted on the wall, and Kai moved to stand there. "We tried to circle around him." She sidestepped a few paces. "But he'd tossed the guards aside and summoned a field of cyclones to hold us off."

Kai lifted his hands, and a dozen cyclones sprouted out of thin air. They twirled completely in sync—moving in that same slow, lazy spin. But unlike Finn and his frenzied cyclones, Kai had his completely under control.

"Is everyone in your family an elemental mage?" she asked.

"Yes. Most of us have additional talents too. Finn is also a summoner, but his summoning isn't any stronger than his casting."

"And what additional talents do you have?"

Magic shone through his eyes, lighting them up. He grinned at her. "Many."

Ok, she'd stepped right into that one. Back to business...

"Finn was making his way toward Building Six," she said.

The cyclones moved with Kai as he walked to Building Six.

"Naomi tossed a few bursts of Dust at him, but the cyclones ate it all up. He started blasting us with wind, trying to hurl us at the fence." She raised her hand quickly. "Don't do that."

"We want to recreate the scene as closely as possible." He looked completely serious. He was ready to blast her across the parking lot. What a psychopath.

"Recreate that part in your head."

"Fine." He dropped his hands. "Keep going."

"Then he threw a fireball at us—don't do that either!"

A sigh brushed past his amused lips as he lowered his half-raised hands.

"He went into a summoning pose and merged all the cyclones into a single spinning wall. But don't you—"

"I told you I had many talents. Summoning is not one of them. So relax."

He drew the tornados in toward him. They blended seamlessly into a wind barrier, twirling in a kaleidoscope of colors. Its spin was silky smooth, its hum whisper soft. A subtle sweetness hung in the air, tickling her tongue. Yum.

Kai had the most beautiful, effortless magic she had ever seen. Magic wasn't something he forced out of himself; it was an extension of his body. It was so breathtaking that she couldn't help but stare.

"How do you do that?" she asked.

"Do what?"

"Make it look so easy."

The wind barrier went nearly transparent. "Practice."

"I've faced a lot of mages. None of them could do what you can. Your cousin was powered by some force that shot his magic up several classes, and even he wasn't this powerful."

Kai turned the barrier light blue. A rim of purple flames sprouted out of the top. It was so beautiful, it was scary. While other mages were sweating trying to make their fire as hot as possible, he was changing its color and forming it into pretty patterns.

"What happened next, Sera?"

"I gave Naomi a boost over the barrier. She landed beside Finn and hit him with some Dust, but for some reason he didn't go down."

"So he gained power and resistance. Go on."

"I couldn't let him finish summoning the dragon. It was gigantic and people would get hurt. I saw a gap in his barrier, so I made a run for it and slipped through."

"Show me."

Crap. "There's no gap in your barrier."

A gap formed in the barrier. It was a crooked circle, perfect in its imitation of chaos. Nature couldn't have designed a better breach if it had tried.

"How about we skip this part, ok?" She walked toward

him. "It was a desperate move, and I got lucky. There's no need to tempt fate."

The flames dissolved into steam, and the wind barrier slid down Kai's body like a silk sheet. He stepped over its fast-fading remains, stopping right in front of her.

"And then?" he asked.

He towered over her, a living wall of muscle and magic. It took every scrap of willpower she had to hold her ground before the dragon. He was looking down at her, his eyes etched with suspicion. One thing was for sure: he wasn't buying her story.

"And then I punched him really hard in the head," she told him.

"Anything else?"

Yes, my body can dissolve other magic on contact. I'm essentially a battering ram against magic. "No, that's it."

Kai turned in place, his eyes scanning the scene. "Something feels wrong here."

The magic-dissolving battering ram standing next to you.

"I can't say exactly what it is. A weird feeling, I guess." He looked at her. "Do you feel it too?"

"There's nothing—" Wait, a minute. Something did smell bad, like slowly rotting magic. Weird.

"You feel it too?"

Sera looked down at the ground. It was humming. The sound was so faint that she hadn't noticed it before.

"Sera?"

A subtle flicker twinkled off the asphalt. She crouched down for a closer look, peeling back layer after layer of magic. It was there. Somewhere.

Suddenly, something shattered, and blue and red drawings faded in. Patterns of swirls and circles and lines covered the ground between Buildings Four and Five.

"They were magically cloaked," Kai said from behind her.

Sera rose, her eyes tracing the peculiar patterns. She'd never seen anything like them before.

"How did you do that?" He set his hand down on her shoulder, then drew it away, shaking it out as though he'd just been burned. "How did you dissolve that cloak? How did you know exactly where the glyphs were? I couldn't even pinpoint them."

There wasn't anything Sera could say that wouldn't make this worse. The best she could hope for was to distract him long enough that she could get away. "Glyphs?"

He took the bait. "Ancient, powerful magic. It's not used by many mages anymore. I recognize these glyphs. They are a gateway."

"You use them to teleport?"

"Yes." He bent down to get a closer look at them.

"Where do they lead to?"

He shook his head. "I don't know. As I said, it's old magic. I've never used it before. I know only what I've read in books."

"Well, now we know how your thieves keep vanishing into thin air."

"So it would seem." He brushed his fingers across one of the glyphs. "There's still magic in these. It's mostly decayed, but there's a little left." He looked up at her. "Sera, I want you to touch these glyphs."

"Why?"

He rose. "When I was in school, my Diagnosis teacher added the Sniffer label to my profile. Do you know what a Sniffer is?"

"Someone who can sense the presence of magic."

"Right. It's like what I was telling you earlier about

monsters being drawn to magic. Some mages can pick up on it too. About one in a hundred can sense it to some degree. And one in a thousand feel magic strongly enough to follow it to its source. They're called Sniffers. My teacher told me I was one of the strongest Sniffers she'd ever seen."

"Just another one of your 'many talents'?"

Kai didn't look amused. "These glyphs were buried under so many cloaking layers that I couldn't find them. You did. I've never felt magic like yours, and we *are* going to talk about it. Right after we figure out where this gateway leads."

Before Sera could come up with an answer to that, a burst of magically-charged lightning split through the sky and crashed down between them. A moment later, a trio of mages stepped onto the parking lot. And they sure didn't look happy to see them.

CHAPTER NINE

Elemental Circus

HALOS OF LIGHTNING and fire encased the three mages. As they walked across the parking lot, a second burst of lightning split through the magically-charged air. Kai bumped Sera aside, lifting his arm to catch the lightning. Blue-purple sparks slid up and down his arm, then fizzled out in his hand.

"You absorbed it," Sera said, her voice cracking.

"The lightning bolt was more flashy than powerful," he replied calmly. "I can absorb low-quality magic."

"What are you calling 'low-quality magic'?" demanded the lightning mage. The tips of her spiky blonde hair sizzled with pink sparks. Her nose ring would have made a bull envious.

The two male mages on either side of her remained silent, their arms folded across their chests. They each wore an identical hoody featuring a peculiar arch over a string of symbols. They could have been sweatshirts from one of the magic fraternities. Their electric companion wore a leather jacket over purposefully torn jeans. From the looks of it, she was the one in charge.

"Either your magic is low quality, or I am a mage you really don't want to cross." Kai shrugged. "Take your pick."

A haughty sneer bounced off her coral lips. "You're in my way, hotshot. Either get lost or get hurt." The sneer spread further up her lips. Electric sparks crackled in her smokey-blue eyes. "Take your pick."

Kai didn't blink. He stepped forward, flipping his hands over. A layer of golden sparks spread out from his palms, quickly consuming his hands.

In response, Miss Lightning arched back, throwing her hands over her head. A swirling ball of electrical energy formed between them, its sparkly tendrils snapping at the air. She hurled it hard at Kai. He ducked, and it smashed into the building behind him, tearing a concrete chunk off the corner.

The hooded mages moved in front of Sera, cutting her off from the lightning duel. In unison, they spread their arms open. Rocks and gravel rose from the ground all around her.

"Telekinetics, huh?" she said.

The mages grinned, manic delight dancing in their eyes. The stony bits formed into a chunky river that began to orbit around the parking lot, like an asteroid belt on earth. Sera looked down at the sword in her hand. It suddenly felt horribly inadequate.

"Step aside," said telekinetic twin number one.

"You are no match for us," added number two.

"You are weak."

"And we are too powerful."

Hit someone hard enough, and they'll go down—well, except maybe a vampire. Damn vampires. Sera hated vampires. They had skulls of steel. Hitting them was like punching a wrecking ball.

Assorted signs tore off the fence and joined into the home-brewed asteroid belt, which continued to spin like the apocalypse was upon them. One of the signs shot out of orbit. Sera ducked, narrowly avoiding what would have been the most bizarre beheading in the history of the world. Rising up again, she glared at the mages. Telekinetics weren't much better than vampires.

"Give up."

"If you want to live."

They sounded like a pair of robotic henchmen out of a cheesy science fiction movie.

"Thanks, but I think I'll take my chances."

Sheathing her sword, Sera picked the battered 'Private Property' sign off the ground, keeping her eyes trained on the twins. Most mages had a dead giveaway that they were about to do magic, even when they were trying to be all stealth about it. In the case of the telekinetic boys, that giveaway was a twitch in their noses that made them look like they seriously had to sneeze.

She eased forward toward them. She made it three steps before Telekinetic Twin Number One's nose wiggled, and a wad of something stony shot out of the belt. She lifted up the sign in front of her, using it as a shield. A hollow, heavy clink echoed as the stone bounced off. She peeked over her shield, only to find a flock of stones swarming toward her.

She looked back at the building, then at the smirking mages in front of her. There wasn't time to be smart; she just had to hope that being fast was good enough. She sprinted for the twins. The stony swarm changed direction to intercept her. Sera pushed herself faster. Her sides burned. Her lungs were screaming out for oxygen. She couldn't stop to give it to them. She stopped, she died. The end.

The swarm dove low and hard. She threw herself forward, stones spitting against the ground, ricocheting at her heels. She landed and rolled, angling toward the twins. If she could just get to them, she'd win. Mages like these—ones who depended on their magic to keep them safe—were total lightweights. They couldn't take a punch. And for the hell they were putting her through, she'd be sure to gift them a few extra punches.

She was almost there. The swarm changed direction again. The backs of her legs felt like they were on fire. The swarm dove. Just a few more steps…

An ice umbrella formed over her head, then spread up like a rainbow, encasing the entire swarm. Sera looked up, her eyes following the frozen arch speckled with stones—then pivoted around to Kai. He was standing over the unconscious lightning mage, brushing snowflakes off his hands. It was a regular elemental circus today.

"You're welcome."

She glared at him.

"Careful there, Sera. When you're upset, your wall cracks. I'm getting a whiff of your magic." He inhaled long and deep. "Mmm. Delicious." He shot her a roguish smile. Which she ignored. Or pretended to, anyway.

"I had it."

"Really? Because it looked to me like you were in distress."

In distress, my ass. "I had it," she ground out, passing under the ice rainbow.

She spun around, launching herself up to slam a kick hard against the twins' heads. One, two, they went down like a pair of dominoes. See? That's what she meant. Total lightweights.

"Good," Kai said as she passed back under the rainbow.

"I'm glad you approve," she said drily.

"Fighting without magic against magical foes certainly has forced you to be creative."

"Yes."

"But you'd make it much easier on yourself if you just used your magic," he said. "Why don't you? What are you afraid of? That you'll get addicted?"

That happened to some mages. They used their powers so much that they turned into magic junkies, always after the next hit. The quest for the next hit quickly escalated into mages going mad, attacking people randomly until the Magic Council sent in a team to deal with the menace. Sometimes, the Magic Council was too slow to act, and that's when scared people started flocking to Mayhem and the other mercenary guilds, begging them to take out the psycho mage well on his way to turning their neighborhood into a post-apocalyptic wasteland.

Sera had once been on a team Simmons had charged with taking out one of these magic junkies—and she had the scars to remember him by. Mages drunk on magic were powerful and resilient. They didn't feel pain like a normal person would. To them, it was just background noise. The power was all that mattered. Using that power was all that mattered. Sort of like Finn when she'd fought him, come to think of it.

"Are you afraid you'll get addicted to the magic?" he repeated.

"No."

"You think you can avoid talking about this. You can't," said Kai.

"Sure I can. Just. Like. This." Sera turned and started to walk away.

"Running away?"

"Walking away."

Behind her, ice roared, and she pivoted around to watch the entire rainbow collapse like a shattered mirror. A million shiny shards rained down on Kai. They burst into flames, dissolving into whiffs of steam before they could touch him.

"What is the matter with you!" she demanded, charging up to him. "Normal people don't act like this. They don't —"

He body-slammed her to the ground, rolling as they fell so that she landed on top of him. Something whistled over their heads.

"What the hell do you think—"

He pressed his finger to her lips, then pointed across the parking lot at the fence that separated his plot from Battery Spencer next door. Magic rippled down the metal web, tearing it from the posts.

"Oh, so you're telekinetic too? Wow, aren't you one special guy." She jumped off of him.

He rose from the ground. "I'm not telekinetic."

"What?"

"I'm not doing that."

"Then who is?"

"I am," a woman's shrill voice sang out.

Sera turned. The mage was standing on top of one of the buildings, her arms extended high to the heavens. Nearby, Miss Lightning stumbled shakily to her feet and pounded her fist against the ground. A river of lightning split across the asphalt, hitting the glyphs, which burst into a halo of glowing light.

The telekinetic swung her arms around, and the metal web shot toward them. A second lightning blast hit Kai in the chest, knocking him back. As he fell toward the shining glyphs, Sera reached out and grabbed his hands, pulling hard.

But the blast was too strong, its momentum sucking her up. They both fell through the glyphs into darkness.

CHAPTER TEN
Falling

SERA HIT THE ground, dirt and pebbles scraping against her bare shoulder as she slid down the hill. She slammed face-first into a spiky bush, which stopped her uncontrolled descent. It also hurt like hell.

A hand caught her around the wrist, pulling her to her feet. She glanced back at Kai. His clothes were neat, his face clean. He certainly didn't look like a tornado had sucked him up and spit him out. How was that even possible? He'd been fighting just like she had.

"You're hurt," he said.

Sera followed his gaze down her legs to the mess that was her jeans. The bottoms were frayed and dirty, and a thick spread of pointy stones had sunk through the fabric and into her calves. That explained the burning sensation that had been steadily growing since the fight.

"I'll be fine."

His eyes narrowed, and his lips drew thin. "How much pain are you in right now?"

None, because I've blocked out most sensation below my knees. "I'll be fine."

"Are you always this stubborn?"

"Yep. Stubborn and rude. That's me."

Sighing, he pointed at a nearby boulder jammed into the hill. "Sit. I'm going to take a look at those wounds."

She considered telling him to shove it, but he was right. She was hurt. If someone else decided to attack them—which, based on how splendidly her day had played out so far, was pretty likely—she'd be next to useless in this state. And if there was one thing she couldn't stand, it was being useless. She could be mature for a few seconds and let Kai take a look at her torn-up legs.

"Will I live?" she asked, wiping the back of her hand across her dusty, sweaty forehead.

Kai looked up from scrutinizing her ruined jeans. "No."

"Thanks."

"You're welcome." He flipped open his pocket knife.

"I hope you're not thinking of amputating anything with that toy."

"If I don't amputate your jeans, your blood will paste them to these puncture wounds."

Resigned to her fate, she waved for him to proceed with the operation. As he began to cut, she kept her eyes high. She didn't need to watch her favorite pair of jeans be butchered. Those mages were going to pay. She didn't know how, but she was going to make sure of that.

"So, we've been transported across the bridge," she said, staring out toward the water. The Golden Gate Bridge shone red-gold in the warm afternoon sun.

"Yes."

Snip. Snip. Snip. The tiny scissors were taking forever, but she supposed they were preferable to her sword.

"At least it wasn't across the country," she added. "If we hurry, maybe those mages will still be there."

He set a hand on her shoulder, pushing her back down onto the boulder. "Remain seated. If you keep going on like this, you'll pass out." He continued cutting away the bottoms of her jeans. "I messaged the facility's security and told them to protect the vault."

"So, did you manage this feat while we were falling through the glyphs or while you were rescuing me from the clutches of that disgruntled bush?"

"Before all that. I wrote to them back outside MRL, demanding to know where the hell they were while we were doing their job. This was right before Olivia arrived on the scene."

"Olivia? Was that the third telekinetic?"

"Yes."

"You know her?"

"She's a member of the Sage Dynasty."

Another of the prominent magic dynasties. Their line wasn't quite as old as the Drachenburgs, but it was old enough. What was a Sage doing helping a group of magical misfits break into Magical Research Laboratories?

"She is being controlled, just like Finn," he answered her unspoken question. "I could see the strange glow in her eyes."

"The drunk-on-magic look."

"That's the one," he said.

"The incidents are related."

"Yes. Whatever Finn was trying to steal, I'll bet Olivia was after the same thing. An attack on the same facility in the span of just a few days by mages with glowing eyes not acting like themselves—that's no coincidence. It's a pattern." He made his final cut, turning her jeans into capris. "Do you have anything to sterilize the wounds?"

Sera shot the ruined strips of denim a despondent look,

then met his eyes. "Of course. I come prepared." She slid a tiny bottle out of a pouch stitched seamlessly into her belt and passed it to him.

"Happen to have a bandage too?" he asked as he took the bottle.

She reached down and slid a roll of gauze out of a second pouch. Kai took it, his hand lingering on hers. For some ridiculous reason, that made Sera's pulse jump. Probably hormones. Those pesky little things were an annoying bunch.

Sera drew her hand away from him. She shouldn't have let him touch her in the first place. The closer he got, the easier it was for him to get a lock on her magic.

"You really do come prepared," he said, cleaning her cuts. "Are you all right?"

Sera winced. "Fine." She'd dropped the wall, allowing the blocked pain to wash through her body. She had to do it sooner or later anyway, and right now the pain was keeping her sensible. It was keeping her from thinking about how magnificent he looked with the sun at his back, lighting him up in a golden halo.

Argh…or maybe not.

"They're not glowing." She pointed at the glyphs etched into the ground. They were fading fast, right before her eyes.

"They pulsed briefly as we fell out of them and have been growing fainter ever since," he told her.

"Have you tried hitting them with magic like the lightning mage did?"

"Yes. While you were busy sliding down the hill, I hit them with a few spells. Nothing happened. Maybe this is just the exit ramp, and the glyphs here are nothing more than a magical residue created by our journey."

"Yeah." She watched the last remnants of the glyphs vanish, leaving behind no evidence that they'd ever been there. She didn't even feel their magic anymore. "We need to get back."

"Yes," he agreed, rising from a crouch. "Ok, you're all set."

Sera looked down. Her best jeans were cut off at the knees. Below that, he'd wrapped up her legs with practiced precision. Not a single bit of gauze was wasted. This wasn't his first time. And that made him unique amongst the mages of the legacy families. Most of them had the first aide skills of a five-year-old. When you had a team of healing mages ready to swoop in every time you stubbed your toe, you tended not to learn the basics of wound treatment.

"Where did you learn to do that?"

"German military."

"Oh."

"You don't believe me?"

"No, a military background totally makes sense for you. It definitely explains your penchant for barking orders and just expecting everyone to follow them."

Something flashed in his eyes. Annoyance? Amusement? The sudden urge to make her his afternoon snack? Did dragons really eat people? The stories said that they did. Sera decided not to think too hard about that. He wasn't a real dragon anyway, just a mage with a dragon's personality. Somehow, that wasn't very comforting.

"So what did you do? In the military, I mean."

"Let's just say I played with tanks."

'Played with tanks'? Yeah, she could totally see that. It fit Kai to a t. Hard-headed. Indestructible. Powerful. A few years ago, there'd been a weapons manufacturer who figured out how to load magically-enchanted ammunition into tanks. It took only one demonstration for all the world's governments to agree on something for a change. Within minutes, there was a worldwide ban on any and all magic ammunition. That didn't mean there wasn't a black market for the stuff, but it was really expensive. And if its price tag wasn't enough to deter most buyers, fear was enough to deter the sellers. The Magic Council frowned upon the sale of unlicensed magic. And you *really* didn't want the Magic Council to ever frown at you.

Sera stood. "Ok, if the glyphs are out, then we'll have to walk it."

"You want to *walk* all the way back? That will take hours."

"Well, what do you want to do? Hitchhike?"

"Walking is not necessary. Nor is hitchhiking. Follow me."

He didn't wait for her to say anything. He just started power-walking down the trail, and Sera had to scramble to catch up. They followed the path to its end, where it spilled out into an open lot bordered on one side by a long brick building. He hurried past the building toward a concrete box that hadn't yet decided if it wanted to be a house or a shed. Inside, he swiped a card through the reader beside the door, then they took the staircase down a level to an underground garage.

The garage could comfortably park twenty cars, but most of the spaces were empty. Two sports cars—one red, one yellow, both egregiously expensive—were parked side-by-side at one end. There was a humble silver minivan somewhere in the middle of the garage. And parked closest to the stairwell was a black SUV that was pretty sleek considering its aspirations to be a tank. Sera wasn't surprised when Kai headed straight for it. The car beeped in greeting.

"It's lucky you happened to park your car right here."

He opened the passenger door for her. "It's not luck. This building belongs to me. And I keep a car in the garage of every building that belongs to me."

Sera climbed up into the car. By the time she had her sword sorted—she didn't think Kai would appreciate her puncturing his upholstery—he was in the driver's seat.

"So, just how many buildings in San Francisco belong to you?" she asked as he turned on the engine.

He drove across the garage and sped up the ramp to shoot out onto the street. "A lot."

And from the look in his eyes, he wasn't even kidding.

CHAPTER ELEVEN

The Priming Bangles

CHAOS REIGNED BACK at Building Six of Magical Research Laboratories. A dozen men in plain black uniforms surveyed the scene, talking into their headsets as they stepped over pulverized concrete. A few of them were clustered around a metal mesh carpet—all that remained of the chain-link fence the telekinetic psychopath had ripped from its posts. As Sera and Kai passed them, she heard them debating what they were going to do about it. Maybe when Olivia regained her senses, she'd offer to magic the fence back on for them.

Kai stopped in front of the guard standing before the doorway to Building Six. "What happened?" His tone was level, but in his eyes brewed a storm of epic proportions. "Where were you while we were doing your job? Oh, let me introduce you to Sera, the only person right now who's earning what I'm paying them."

Since he was clearly having a moment, she didn't mention that he hadn't actually paid her anything yet. She did, however, extend her hand to the poor guard he was barbecuing with his glare.

"Sera, this is Dawson," he continued as Dawson shook her hand. "Now explain why you didn't come running up the stairs the moment the facility was attacked."

"We were stuck."

"Stuck?"

Dawson had turned a tad green. "Yes. Someone melded shut the door to the guardhouse. It took Gin half an hour to melt a big enough hole in it for us to climb out. By the time we made it upstairs, the fight was over. The mages were gone. And so were you."

"We fell through some glyphs that transported us to the other side of the bridge," Sera told him.

He chewed that over for a moment, then said, "I didn't know that sort of magic exists."

"Today is a big day for firsts," Kai cut in. "Like my guards getting themselves locked in. Did you at least see something on the security feeds from there?"

"Yes. After you disappeared, Olivia Sage and several others stepped into Building Six. And then all the feeds went blank."

Sera looked at Kai. "Just like during all your other break-ins."

"From the look on your face, I take it they made it past my security measures. What did they steal?" he asked Dawson.

"The Priming Bangles."

Confusion loosened Kai's tight jaw, chiseling away at some of his anger. "Why would they steal those?"

"I don't know, sir."

"What are Priming Bangles?" Sera asked.

"Two pairs of gold bracelets."

"And this is what whoever is behind all this was after? This is why they've broken into so many of your company's facilities?"

"I don't know. The bracelets are pretty. And they're made with gold, rubies, and sapphires. So they're quite valuable from monetary perspective," said Kai. "But they're not especially magical. Very low grade magic."

"What do they do?"

"They help young or inexperienced mages focus their power. For centuries, children in the Drachenburg family have used them during their early years, when their magic was starting to blossom."

"Did you use them?"

"No." He looked offended. "They're for our underpowered and undisciplined children, the ones who need a jolt to bring forth their magic. The child wears one pair, and a more experienced mage wears the other, using the bracelets to help the child direct his magic."

"I've never heard of anything like that."

"Our set is the only one of its kind," he replied. "But I still don't understand why someone would go to so much trouble to steal it. We created the bangles to deal with mages of feeble magic born into the family line. We had to find some way to give them a boost. We couldn't have any Drachenburg weak mages running around."

Sera frowned at him. "Yeah, because that would be totally embarrassing."

"It would be dangerous. Being a weak mage born into a powerful family makes you a target of that family's enemies. Or pirates and scoundrels looking to make their fortune kidnapping members of wealthy families."

"Oh." Her hands slid down from their perch on her hips.

"But here's the thing. The bracelets don't give a mage power he doesn't possess. They just teach him to draw on every bit of magic in him. Most mages can access only a fraction of their total magic."

"How much?"

"Under half. Usually a third or even a quarter."

"And these bracelets allow mages to draw on all their potential magic?"

"Not quite. It's not a panacea for low magic. A mage can't put them on and suddenly have access to all this magic he couldn't get to before. It takes years of conditioning, and you have to start young, ideally before puberty," he said. "Any one of the other dynasties would love to get their hands on our bangles to use them on their own unpowered children, but they wouldn't go about it so directly. And it's not thieves after the bangles because by now whoever is behind this has spent more money trying to steal them than they are worth on the black market."

"What if something else was stolen too?" Sera suggested. "What if they weren't after these bracelets at all?"

"But used that to cover up something else they'd stolen." He turned to Dawson. "Are you sure the Priming Bangles were the only item stolen?"

"The team that took inventory said everything else is still there," replied Dawson. He'd looked happier back when Kai was ignoring him.

"Do it again. You personally. Start now. I expect a report by the morning."

Alone, that would probably take him half the night, but he didn't protest. He didn't say a word. He just nodded, turned, and walked down the stairs into the underground building. Sera waited until he was out of earshot before telling Kai off.

"You could've had someone help him. It's not his fault the guard house was sabotaged."

"I'm not punishing him," he said. "I want him to do it because I'm not entirely sure there aren't spies and traitors amongst us. I can't afford to trust the other guards."

"But you can afford to trust him?"

"Yes."

"Why?" she asked, even though she was sort of—uh, make that really, absolutely certain she didn't want to know.

Kai just looked at her, saying nothing.

"That bad?"

"Let's just say that Dawson has seen what happens to people who betray me," he said, cold fury in his eyes.

A bolt of lightning shot down from the sky, blasting a garbage can clear across the parking lot. As it fell, flames consumed the metal, melting it into a shapeless blob even before it hit the ground. Wow. And, oh yeah, holy shit.

"Should I be worried that you're going to set me on fire?" she asked him.

"It depends. Are you going to betray me?"

"I wasn't planning on it."

"Good. I'd stick to that plan if I were you."

The look in his eyes told her he wasn't joking. If she did something he saw as a threat, he'd barbecue her on the spot, no questions asked, no mercy granted. The problem was that her very existence was something he'd see as a threat.

"Let's go," he said, heading toward his car. "We have one more stop to make before we can call it a day and start again tomorrow."

"What is it?"

"You'll see."

She tried not to let the delighted grin on his face worry her.

CHAPTER TWELVE

Dragon Born

WHERE DID EGREGIOUSLY wealthy dragons get their grub? From posh restaurants that verified your bank account balance at the door, of course. Ok, not really, but it was pretty damn close.

Illusion was one of these restaurants. It sat along the shore of the Presidio, the city kingdom for the magically inclined. And it was all 'pretty' magic here in the Presidio. No beasts in sight—well, not unless you counted the three-headed dogs and acid-spitting toads that guarded the gates of the magical elite. Truth be told, they weren't half as bad as the monsters holding their leashes.

Kai led the way through the door, stepping foot into that restaurant like he owned the place. Which was actually a distinct possibility, come to think of it.

"Is this yours?" Sera whispered as the host walked over, his steps hurried yet smooth.

"Is what mine?"

"This restaurant."

"No, of course not. Owning a restaurant would take all the pleasure out of eating there."

"Mr. Drachenburg, it's a pleasure to see you again," the host said. He was wearing a tuxedo. And a spiffy watch that Sera could have pawned off to buy herself a pretty awesome pair of boots. "Your usual table is set and ready for you. Shall I show you and your companion there now?"

Sera had to give it to Mr. Fancy Tuxedo. He didn't even blink at her dirty top and torn jeans. Maybe Kai came in looking like this all the time. Well, at least there wasn't blood dripping from her sword or monster guts on her shoes.

At Kai's nod, the host showed them into the dining area. Here, the name of the game was opulence. The floors were cherrywood, the tablecloths silk, and the guests sparkling with enough diamonds to send a Christmas tree into an epileptic seizure.

Those guests weren't as courteous as the Illusion host. Not only did they blink, they gawked. Copiously. Every head in the room turned to watch Sera and Kai cross the room. She tried to ignore them—but only sort of succeeded. Disdain dripped from their faces like molasses. Apparently, they didn't approve of the denim and leather invasion. Or maybe it was the dirt and dried blood.

"Are we here to meet someone about the case?" Sera asked Kai.

"We're here to eat. It's been a long day, and I'm hungry."

He stepped in front of the host to slide Sera's chair out for her. Sore, wounded, and plain worn out, she plopped down. It felt good to sit. She ran her hands across the seat. Mmm, leather. And not of the battle wear variety either. Sitting in that chair felt as good as sinking into a hot bubble bath. It was the most heavenly seat she'd ever met.

Across from her, Kai plucked a roll from the basket.

Steam wafted up from it, the scent of freshly baked bread unfurling from its tasty flesh. Sera grabbed a roll for herself and made quick work of it.

"Butter?" Kai held out a tray, an amused smile light on his lips.

She took it from him, spreading the garlic butter generously across her second roll. After she finished her third, she hazarded a peek at the other guests in the dining area. They were still gawking. Geez.

She leaned forward, whispering to him, "Everyone is staring at us."

"Let them stare." He didn't whisper. He projected his voice, its rich bass filling the room. "The vast majority of them have nothing better to do anyway. Our arrival is the most interesting thing that has happened to them in weeks." He looked down at the bread basket, frowning when he found it empty. "Besides, if they don't stop staring, I'll roast them and eat them for dinner. As I said, I'm famished."

Clothing rustled and silverware clinked as the gawkers hastily looked away.

"You cannot be serious," Sera said as a team of waiters refilled their water glasses and set down fresh baskets of bread and other appetizers.

"Sure, I am." He popped a cube of something lightly breaded into his mouth. "I'm a dragon."

Ha! I knew it! Except there weren't any dragons anymore. "You look like a mage to me."

"Ok, so maybe I'm not a *real* dragon, but I do shift into one."

Sera's knife slipped from her hand, clinking against her plate. *Holy-moly recycled zombie parts, that's why he's so powerful.*

"You dropped your weapon."

She righted the knife.

"What's wrong? Haven't you ever met a dragon shifter before?" His smile was smug, like he knew exactly where in the food chain he sat. Hell, he was flying so high above the food chain that it was only a tiny speck to him.

Sera forced herself to speak, to say anything. It wasn't wise to let a predator know he'd stunned you. "No, as a matter of fact, I haven't."

A small subset of mages could shift their shape. These mage shifters were rare and usually stuck to human forms and the simpler animals, things like birds or mice. Some first tier mages could manage one of the big cats or even a bear. As far as Sera knew, there hadn't been a dragon shifter in over a century. It took an enormous amount of magic to shift into the most magical of all beings: the dragon. Like mind-blowing amounts of magic.

She had to be careful around him—very, very careful. If he found out what she was, he would kill her, or at least bring her before the Magic Council. And she didn't think she was strong enough to stop him. Not that she wouldn't try.

"No? You haven't met a dragon shifter before? Well, I guess I shouldn't be surprised. At the moment, there are only two of us in the world, and the other is a monk at a secluded Tibetan monastery." He inhaled deeply, keeping his eyes fixed on her. "Uncommon as we are, we're not unique. Not like you. I've never met anyone like you before. You are special."

Sera knew he was trying to scent out her magic—again—and there wasn't much she could do about it, except to stuff it down where he'd hopefully never find it. Too bad dragons had a nose for magic. She did too. That was just part of being Dragon Born.

Despite its name, the Dragon Born didn't have much to do with dragons. In fact, Kai's magic was closer to the dragons' than hers was. The Dragon Born got their name from the unique circumstance of their birth: they were two souls born into one body, later separated by magic. Just like how the dragons were born.

Long ago, the Dragon Born were, if not common, at least a part of the world. A handful were born into each generation, and they were the most powerful mages of their time. It was an unexpected side effect of the separation spell. When the two souls were split into two bodies, their magic didn't divide—it multiplied. Each new mage had the power of two.

Or so the legends told. Sera didn't know if any of it were true. All she did know was that at some point in history, the rest of the supernatural world had turned against the Dragon Born, branding them abominations. They were killed at birth. And for those who escaped an early execution, a later one awaited them. The minute the Magic Council got word of their existence, they turned the world upside down to get to them.

Sera and her sister Alex were Dragon Born. As soon as their parents had realized that, they'd taken the whole family into hiding. And they'd been hiding ever since. Dad had died to protect them. And their mother… Well, Sera didn't even remember her. She was probably dead too. Dad had never talked much about her, as though the memory of her hurt too much.

Sera didn't know why the Magic Council had turned against the Dragon Born, but it probably came down to fear. They feared what they didn't understand—and couldn't control. The stories of the Dragon Born told of magic Sera couldn't even begin to comprehend, let alone wield. She knew her and Alex's magic felt different than other people's, but it certainly wasn't powerful. She could sense magic. She could hide it. And she could break it. None of that was especially spectacular, at least not as spectacular as throwing fireballs, shattering windows with telekinetic blasts, or shifting into an extinct magical beast. And the Magic Council hadn't outlawed any of those kinds of magic.

Across from Sera, Kai was shaking his head. "I don't recognize your magic. All I can say is that you're definitely not human."

She and Alex had spent their whole lives masquerading as human, and he was only the second person who hadn't bought the act.

"You've gone quiet," Kai said.

What to say, what to say... "I didn't think dragons liked bread." *Ugh, definitely not that stupid comment.*

Kai gave her a grin worthy of a fire-breathing predator. "That's right. Dragons like meat." He looked straight at the duo of waiters standing nearby, and they swooped in. "I'll take the Kobe steak. Medium rare."

As one of them hurried off, the other looked at Sera.

"Uh..." She flipped through the menu, searching in vain for something with a price tag under three digits. "... Ok, the mushroom soup."

There wasn't anything else on the menu she could afford. Honestly, she couldn't even afford the soup, at least not without eating ramen for the next week. Oh, joy, ramen, the one thing even magic couldn't make taste better.

"I hope you aren't one of those women who starves herself to fit into a dress," Kai said, his voice heavy with disapproval.

"My dresses fit just fine, thank you," she replied. *All one of them.*

He didn't look appeased. Or amused.

"Fine, it's because I'm broke. I have no money to waste on fancy dishes I can't even pronounce," she admitted. "Happy now?"

"No, I am most certainly not happy. You need to eat," he told her. "Don't worry about the cost. You're on the clock. You can bill your meal to me."

"In that case, I may just order a salad with my soup."

"Hold on now, before you do something really crazy." He looked at the waiter. "Scrap the salads and soups. Bring her a steak."

"Now just *you* hold on. I am perfectly capable of ordering on my own," she protested.

"No, you're really not. You need real food, not rabbit food. I can't have you passing out in the middle of a fight." He waved the waiter away. "It's not healthy the way you live. And it doesn't make any sense. You have magic. A lot of it." He held up his hand, stopping her emerging protest. "With your magic, you could make so much more money, and yet you do everything in your power to make sure you remain a bottom of the barrel mercenary. Why? You're clearly hurting for money, and there's a definite path open to you to alleviate this problem. I'm familiar with Mayhem's payment tiers. All you'd have to do is march into Simmons's office and fess up that you have magic. Once you were tested, your pay rank would jump from the bottom right up to the top. That I can guarantee."

"Why do you even care? My money—or lack thereof—is my problem."

An agitated wrinkle formed between his eyes. "You're being absurd."

"Then let me be absurd. It's *my* problem. I don't want to talk about it," she said. "And you have a very overinflated view of my magic." She nudged the roll across her plate, putting on a cheery smile. "I'm a mushroom, remember?"

"No." Kai reached forward and seized her hand, freezing it before she could continue fiddling with her food. His skin was hot, like it had been forged in a volcano. He looked her right in the eye. "You're not."

Sera wasn't sure how to respond to that, but the waiter saved the day. He'd returned with two plates, an enormous steak upon each. And by enormous, she meant this-could-feed-a-small-mercenary-team enormous. She drew her hand away from Kai's and picked up her silverware. Eating was a good way to avoid talking. Kai was already eating; he'd met the arrival of his dinner with great enthusiasm. But through it all, his eyes never left her. He stared across the table at her, as though he was plotting something. They ate in silence.

When he'd devoured the steak, he waved over the waiter so he could order dessert. The waiter turned to her, but she just shook her head.

"I'm full."

"Bring a second slice of cheesecake," Kai told him, and the waiter scurried off.

Sera resisted the urge to draw her sword. "I said I was full."

"You did." He didn't get it.

"Why are you such a control freak? What gives you the right to decide what's best for everyone?" She tried to keep her tone level, but, yeah, he was really starting to piss her off.

He met her glower with a calm smile. "When the cake comes, and you still don't want it, then I'll just eat yours too."

Whatever. This was all a game to him, and she would not play along. The waiter returned with their dessert: two slices of cheesecake with a chocolate crust and raspberries on top. It looked good—maybe even good enough to make her forget she was stuffed. But she wasn't about to give Kai the satisfaction. He was already watching her with a smug smirk on his face, like he knew she wanted it. He leaned in toward her, magic rolling off of him, flooding her, filling her with heat…

He froze, and the magic snapped back into him. His eyes looked past her shoulder. "Our man has arrived."

"What?" She shivered. The sudden withdrawal of his magic had left her cold.

"Harrison Sage," he said. "Olivia's brother. He's just sitting down. Five tables behind you."

Sera didn't look. She didn't need to. She could feel him back there; his magic felt very similar to Olivia's. He wasn't a telekinetic, but their magic shared that same familial undercurrent.

"I thought we were here to eat," she said.

"We can do both," he replied as he stood. "Come on. Let's go pay him a visit."

She followed him to Harrison's table. This time, no one gawked at them as they crossed the room—at least not openly. What thoughts were spinning around in their heads she didn't know but could easily guess. She'd tromped across their fancy restaurant in muddy shoes and jeans cut off at the knees. Her lower legs were wrapped in bandages, her arms tattooed with scratches. Dirt, sweat, and dried blood were competing for prominence on her top, and her hair looked like she'd jammed her finger into an electrical socket.

"Harrison," Kai greeted the mage. "Fancy meeting you here."

He dipped his chin in response. "Kai. How are things? How's business?"

"Profitable."

Harrison's smile was perfect, his tone practiced. "Really? I'd heard you were having problems. A series of break-ins?"

Yeah, the two of them totally despised each other. Maybe they'd once fought over the same magical toy.

"It's funny you should mention that," said Kai. "Because we've just had another one this afternoon."

"Oh, really? Sorry to hear that."

"And the incursion was led by your sister."

Harrison snorted. "Are you sure that was an 'incursion' and not just Olivia being moody? You know how she gets sometimes. Maybe you annoyed her."

"She blasted me through a glyph that transported me clear across the Golden Gate Bridge," Kai said drily.

Harrison laughed. "Yeah, you annoyed her all right."

Kai gave him the dragon's grin. You know, the one a poor, unsuspecting sap got before becoming dinner. The smile died on Harrison's lips.

"We aren't talking about a silly prank like the one she once pulled with the multiplying fireworks over New York. This is hardcore, ancient magic. And Olivia used it to get me out of the way so she could steal from me. If you don't do something about her, I will. And trust me when I say, she won't like it."

"There's no need for threats. I'll pay you for whatever she took."

"I don't want your money. I want my property returned to me."

"I'll look into it."

Harrison was such a bad liar. Kai picked up on that as well. His expression hardened.

"What do you know about all this?"

"I?" He pretended to look surprised. "Nothing."

Liar, liar, pants on fire. His magic had shifted pitch when he'd lied. It was practically screaming inside Sera's ears.

Kai glared down at him, then his eyes swept the room. A trio of bodyguards stood nearby, watching the exchange.

"I'll be in touch," Kai told Harrison, then turned and walked away.

"He's lying," Sera whispered as they made their way to the entrance hall.

"Later," he said, low and quiet.

He paid, and they left the restaurant, each with a boxed dessert in their hands. Kai waited until they were in his car and driving off down the street before speaking.

"You're right. He is lying. He's always been an atrocious liar. His magic tingles when he lies," he said. "He knows something about the theft."

"But what?" Sera asked. She didn't mention that she'd felt the very same thing from Harrison's magic.

"I don't know. But I will find out. That I guarantee."

CHAPTER THIRTEEN

Legacy of Magic

SERA'S APARTMENT WAS only about a ten-minute drive away from Illusion, but they might as well have been worlds apart. Pristine lawns on enormous upscale estates gave way to blocks of cute little row houses and apartment buildings. The dividing line between San Francisco's magical playground and the real city couldn't have been more obvious if they'd planted the Great Wall of China at the border.

Sera sat in the passenger seat of Kai's tank, her fingertips crunching into the cake box on her lap. She gazed out the window, her eyes unfocused—and more importantly, not looking at him. She could still feel him beside her, his magic bubbling just below the surface. It unrolled, inching toward her in slow, pulsing breaths.

"Stop that," she growled as his magic brushed across her neck.

"Why?"

"Because I find it annoying."

He sniffed the air. "Your magic would seem to indicate otherwise."

Damn. No matter what she did to mask her magic, he always saw right through her. When she got home, she'd have some serious reading to do. Maybe she'd find something to help her in one of Dad's old magic books.

"You like my magic," Kai continued. "And your magic likes my magic."

"No," she lied. His magic snapped and sizzled and burned—and not even in a bad way. When it touched her, adrenaline and endorphins hooked up and threw a wild party in her body.

"Right." A smirk spread across his lips, smug and overbearing. He slid his hand across the armrest toward her.

"Touch me and I'll retaliate."

His smile widened. "That might be worth it."

"I mean it. I have a knife, and I'm pretty good at using it. So unless your magic includes the ability to regrow fingers, I'd keep it and the rest of you away from me."

He retracted his hand, but the look in his eyes told her that her threat hadn't repelled him. Just the opposite actually; it had enticed him. Why? Oh, that's right. Because he was a freaking psychopath. Just like the rest of the magical elite.

"Sera—"

"What do you think Harrison Sage knows?"

Kai's gaze flicked to her, then back to the road. Thank goodness. The last thing she needed was to end the night in a ditch. Probably hacking her way through an army of zombies too, knowing her luck.

"Either Harrison's protecting his sister, or he's involved too," Kai said. "I hope it's not the latter. That would be a phenomenal pain in the ass."

"Why?"

"He has a seat on the Magic Council."

Sera couldn't say she was surprised, what with Harrison's stellar personality, but she was worried. She'd made it her goal in life to stay as far away from the Magic Council as she possibly could.

"As you saw, he has power and resources. And bodyguards." Kai snorted, and smoke puffed out of his nostrils. "Fine, he's not a top fighter, but the guards just make him look weak."

"I see… Um, did you know your nose is on fire?"

He patted down the flames. "That happens sometimes." There was something awfully eerie about the casual way that he said it.

"So, what kind of mage is Harrison?"

"A summoner mainly, his favorite summons being unicorns, eagles, and vampires. I bet you didn't know you can summon a vampire."

"I did actually," she said. "I fought a crew of them once. And barely survived. Killing summoned vampires is about as easy as trying to decapitate a mosquito with a sword. It's a good thing I'd brought along a flamethrower."

His face went completely serious. "Look, if you ever get bored working for Simmons, I'll double whatever he's paying you."

Walk willingly into the mouth of the dragon? I don't think so. "If you're nice to me, I promise to think about it."

"You're lying."

"Yes."

"I think I can change your mind."

I seriously doubt it. "You're welcome to try."

Sera was kicking herself even before she saw the spark in his eyes. She had not just taunted the dragon with an impossible challenge. Except that she had. Because she'd lost her mind. Taunting dragons was bad. Bad, bad, bad.

"Um, let's just get back to the Harrison issue." She cleared her throat. "You were saying he likes to summon unicorns, eagles, and vampires."

"Among other things." He was watching her strangely, like he half-expected her to jump through the window. "Harrison never did master dragons, though. And he's pretty sour about it too."

"Because the summoners in your family can summon dragons," she guessed.

"Of course they can. It's all in the name."

"So I take it 'Drachenburg' means crazy dragon people who go on long and fiery rampages?"

He laughed. "Something like that. Dragons are the pinnacle of summoning. And Harrison cannot stand failing."

"What magic can he do besides summoning?"

"He can cast a handful of elemental spells," replied Kai. "Olivia is the stronger mage, but she's too unstable for the Sage family to put her in the driving seat. She'd drive their legacy right into the ground just because it sounded like a funny idea at the time."

"And did your family put you in the driving seat?"

"For some things. Mostly the business side. My parents still control the rest."

"What about your siblings?"

"I don't have any. My extended family is large, though. Dozens of cousins."

"And you're the oldest of them?"

"No, just the most responsible. I'm not *that* old, you know."

Sera knew she shouldn't, but curiosity won out. "How old are you?"

"Thirty."

Not so many years older than she was.

"You're surprised," Kai said. "Do I look so old?"

No. "Yes."

He chuckled as he turned into the parking lot. "Where can I park?"

"Anywhere. Most of us who live here don't have cars."

"How do you get around?"

"With the bus. Or my scooter." She frowned at him. "Why are you laughing?"

"I'm picturing you explaining to the bus driver that you don't, in fact, plan to massacre every living soul on his bus with that big sword you carry around."

"Plenty of people bring their gear onto public transportation. I have a license for the sword, and I always carry my Mayhem badge. People are actually relieved to see it because it means they're safe as long as I'm traveling with them. If members of the vampire mafia try to hijack the bus, I've got it covered."

He turned off the engine. "Has that ever happened?"

"No," she said as they both stepped out of the car.

She followed the cobbled path past a lonely picnic bench and a dusty patch of dirt in the grass that the neighborhood winged cat liked to use as a litter box. All the tenants did their part in cleaning up after the stray. If you let winged cat poop sit too long in the sun, it combusted. And spread fast. Entire cities had caught on fire thanks to a few magical cat droppings.

San Francisco was one of them. The disaster of 1906? That was all thanks to a magic-drunk elemental mage and a whole lot of winged cat poop. Not that the general population knew the truth. They all believed that earthquake story propagated by the Magic Council.

"I don't need an escort," Sera told Kai, who was keeping

pace beside her.

"Last time I was here, vampires attacked. I feel obliged to at least check under your bed for monsters this time around."

"You are not going anywhere near my bed."

"Fine. You can check for monsters under my bed."

She'd been reaching for the doorknob when her hand dropped out of the air, like a harpy who'd just been firebombed. "Are you propositioning me?"

"Are you accepting?" He sure looked serious, and he had such a tight wrap on his magic that Sera couldn't tell if he was lying. "Today was fun."

"Fun?" Now she knew he must be messing with her. "Which part? The battle at MRL, being teleported across the bridge, or the arrogant prick at the restaurant?"

"All of it," he said. "I should get out of the office more often. I should hang out with fun people more often. I can't tell you what a relief it is to be around another normal person for a change."

Normal? Neither of them was the least bit normal. Potent and ancient, his magic was off the charts. And she… Well, she was an abomination, right?

"You consider yourself normal, do you?" she asked.

"No, I'm a bloodthirsty psychopath. Just like you."

He leaned in, his arms braced against the doorframe, his eyes burning with need. Sera could almost see the dragon peeking out from behind the man. The dragon was powerful, seductive, and ruthless. It was wrapped in a magic as old as the world itself.

"Speak for yourself." She suppressed a shudder as his magic slid over her shoulders, sending rivers of liquid heat down her back. "Hey, I told you to knock that off."

"Your lips say one thing. Your magic says another." His

whispered words caressed her cheek. "And right now it's singing."

"For you to stop," she breathed out. Yeah, breathing. That was getting hard.

"You don't want me to stop."

No, she really didn't. But right now she was suffering from very poor judgement. She shoved out her hands to push him away. He hopped back, laughing.

"Is that the best you can do?" he taunted.

"No." She swung a punch at him, aiming for that arrogant smirk.

She missed.

He pivoted out of her way, flicking her on the back as she passed by him. "Too slow."

She spun around to hit him again, but he ducked. He was fast. Just not fast enough. Adrenaline pumping in her ears, she pounded her fists down hard on his head.

"Damn it, Sera," he growled, stumbling back. "That hurt."

But he was still standing. Anyone else would have had the decency to pass out. Not the dragon, though. Oh, no. He was far too stubborn.

She swung another punch at him, but he caught her hand and twisted it behind her back. "Let go."

"I'm not holding you very tightly. You could break free." He leaned in closer. "But you haven't." His lips brushed against hers, teasing her with promises of more. "Why is that?"

"Because you're my client." She nipped his lip. "I can't attack you or else—"

Kai pulled her against him, swallowing her words whole. His tongue plunged into her open mouth, his kiss hard and urgent. His magic wasn't wrapped away—not anymore. It slammed and smashed against hers, saturating her every pore. She knew this was a really, really, *really* bad idea, and she just didn't care. She wanted to drown in his magic and never come up for air.

Floodlights blared down, blasting her with blinding light. Except it wasn't floodlights, her mind was trying to tell her. It was the porch light. Something clinked and jiggled. Metal. The door! Sera pushed back from Kai, landing on the doormat as the door opened. Riley looked out at her.

"What are you doing out here, standing all alone in the dark?" he asked.

Sera looked around. Kai was nowhere in sight. She heard the rumble of an engine and tires crinkling over gravel as a car drove out of the parking lot. Wow, he sure moved fast.

"Did you lose your keys?" Riley asked.

"No," she said wearily. The insanity of the day was finally catching up to her, and she was crashing.

Riley's eyes narrowed as his eyes took in the blood-dried bandages, the torn-off jeans, and whatever else was wrong with her. She hadn't looked in a mirror in hours, which was a good thing.

"Sera, what happened to you?" He frowned. "You look like shit."

"Thanks. I love you too," she said, slipping past him to go inside. "It's been a long day. I'm going to shower and call it a night."

"Wait."

She stopped her tired shuffle down the hall and looked back at him.

"What's that?"

He pointed at the doormat. There, beside the potted

lavender plant sat the two cake boxes, stacked one on top of the other. Sera took a step back and swept them up into her arms. She gave the boxes a hard glare. Cats dumped dead mice on your doorstep. Maybe dragons left you cake. Kai was making a power play, marking his territory or some other such dragon nonsense.

Yeah, so that wasn't happening. She handed the boxes off to Riley.

"Here. I brought you cheesecake. Enjoy."

He peeked inside, then shot her a grin. "Sweet! I haven't eaten yet. Thanks."

"You're welcome," Sera said.

And as she trudged down the hall toward the bathroom, she wondered what the hell she was going to do about that dragon.

CHAPTER FOURTEEN
Magic Smoothies

THE NEXT MORNING, Sera slept in until ten. Then she changed into her workout clothes, pulled her hair up into a high ponytail, and headed for the kitchen. She gave Riley's door a good morning thump along the way.

"Rise and shine, sleeping beauty!"

A string of muffled curses came from the closed door.

"Hey, you were the one who wanted to run with me," she reminded him. "I'll be heading out in half an hour. You snooze, you lose. And losers get dishwashing duty."

Something hit the door. It sounded like a pillow.

"That's nice. But I suggest you save your energy for the trail. You'll need it when you're eating my dust."

A second pillow smacked the door. Then the bed creaked, and two feet landed hard on the floor. Satisfied that he was conscious enough to at least zombie-walk his way to the bathroom for a wakeup shower, Sera continued on to the kitchen. She poured herself a full bowl of granola and sat down with a stack of magic books.

She skimmed the index of each book for instructions on how to mask her magic, but came up short. She'd already read everything they had and then some on the topic. It was the very first skill Dad had taught her and Alex, and they'd spent over two decades perfecting it. It had never failed. Never. Until she'd met Kai. He was the only one who'd ever been able to sense her magic. She didn't even know what to do about him. It was probably too late anyway. The damage was done. She'd just have to make sure no one else ever found out—and hope Kai didn't spill the beans.

After texting a note to Riley to read up on masking magic at his school library, she moved on to the glyphs. This time, she fared better, finding a few passages about the ancient symbols in two different books. By the time she had read through them all, she'd finished her breakfast. She typed the key points about glyphs into her phone, then went to the sink to wash out her bowl.

Her cell phone buzzed. She took one look at the number, then hit ignore.

The home phone rang. The call was from a funny number with lots of digits. Safe. Sera swiped it off the stand.

"Hey, Alex."

"Sera. Did I wake you?"

"No, I just finished breakfast and was about to head out for a run." She fiddled with the peeling corner of the cheap kitchen table they used only for breakfast. "How are you?"

"Busy."

"Are you still in Zurich?"

"Yep. Look, things are super crazy right now. It looks like I'm going to be here much longer than I'd thought. Will you and Riley be all right for awhile without me?"

Translation: I'm having a blast hunting supernatural baddies, while being free to party and do whatever carefree people do, and I don't want to come back.

"Sure. I'll try to remember to feed him when he gets hungry."

Silence hissed from the other end of the line for a few seconds before Alex said, "After I get back, we'll go hunt down some nasty monster who's wrecking havoc on the city."

If she ever came back. Mayhem had flown Alex across a freaking ocean because the world's most famous supernatural had asked for her. Gaelyn. He was the first immortal. People said he was over six thousand years old, though no one knew for certain. One thing was for sure, though: the ancient immortal was as rich as he was old. And Alex worked for him now. When she was finished with whatever task he'd given her, would she want to return to their mundane life? Sera had heard there were balls in Europe. She'd always wanted to go to a ball. If this were a fairytale, her fairy godmother would swoop in and turn her cutoff jeans and torn shirt into a magnificent gown, then whisk her off to the ball.

But life was no fairytale. Any ball she managed to find herself at would include dancing zombies and a swarm of hungry vampires. Well, admittedly she'd landed a prestigious assignment too. Unfortunately, it had come with an arrogant dragon.

"Nasty monsters. Sounds like fun," Sera said.

"Is Riley there?"

"He's in the shower."

"Give him a kiss for me. I'll give you a call again soon. I have to run now. "

"Take care of yourself, Alex."

"You too."

Just as Sera set down the phone, Riley emerged from

the bathroom, dressed in his running clothes. She forced a cheery smile onto her face.

"You're five minutes late, hotshot."

"Relax." He grabbed a bagel. "Was that Alex?"

Sera nodded. "She sounds like she's having fun."

"So are you."

"How do you figure that?"

"I saw the look on your face last night. Whatever crazy, wild, dangerous shenanigans you went through yesterday sure put you in a great mood."

"Crazy, wild, dangerous shenanigans?"

"Yep." He chomped down on his bagel. "You love crazy, wild, dangerous shenanigans. The crazier, wilder, and more dangerous—the better."

"That's not true."

"Sure it is."

"Not."

"Is."

This could go on forever. Sera pointed at the clock. "Seven minutes late."

Riley stuffed the remainder of his bagel into his mouth, then headed for the door.

Sera and Riley ran side-by-side in silence, the heat of a cloudless sky blaring down on them. They never chitchatted while running. There would be plenty of time to do that later, when they weren't racing to be the first to the little waterfront smoothie bar where they often paused to partake in fruity treats.

Sera's cadence was off today. Her legs still hurt from yesterday's dance with the telekinetics. She'd removed the gauze, replacing it with a field of smaller patches, but below the skin, her muscles ached.

Physical ailments aside, the real reason she was so slow today was that her mind just wasn't in it. She'd long ago trained herself to push through physical pain, but apparently all it took was a dragon in her head to keep her mind off the game.

What was she going to do about him? The smart, rational thing to do was stay well away from him. He came from one of the elite magic dynasties, and he could somehow sense her magic, no matter what she did to cover it. One of those two things alone would be reason enough to keep her distance. Both together should have had her running for the hills. He represented everything she'd spent her whole life hiding from. He was bad news and lots of it.

And yet there was something about him, something she found herself drawn to. The song of his magic was incredible, the feel of it crashing against her simply divine. She'd had only the tiniest taste of it, but that had been enough. She wanted more. She wanted him to kiss her as he poured his magic into her, saturating her body until it hummed and tingled in tune with his.

Where the hell did all that come from?

Sera pushed herself to run faster, trying to squeeze those insane thoughts out of her head. She couldn't let herself want those things from Kai because she had a feeling he'd give them to her and then some. And after that, she'd never be able to get him out of her head. She had to stop this now, while she still could.

Even as her muscles screamed in protest, she upped the pace again. Beside her, Riley's breaths grew strained and shallow. Sweat streamed down the sides of Sera's face. It slid along her neck and plunged down her back.

As they neared the water, the air cooled, and a light breeze rolled off her sweat-beaded skin. Sera could almost taste the strawberry sweetness. The swirly shop sign came into sight, and that was all the motivation she needed. She shot forward, running all out the rest of the way there.

It wasn't only mages who partook in the joy that was magic smoothies. A sizable chunk of the human population ordered them too. So it didn't look the least bit suspicious for Sera to step up to the counter and order a pair of them for her and Riley.

"Did Alex have any news?" Riley asked.

They stood outside at a banana-yellow table beneath a strawberry umbrella, slurping magic-boosted smoothies through super thick straws. Ice crystals slid down Sera's throat, dissolving the heat trapped inside her body. A subtle magic aftertaste tingled her tongue.

"Not really. Just that she's really busy," Sera said. "She sounds like she's having a blast."

"It's good for her to get out and see new things. The two of you have spent so many years hiding, working, and looking out for me. It's no life. You need to *live* life and not worry about me so much."

"It's our fault Dad died. Our fault that you had to grow up without him."

"I was fourteen. I'd already done most of my growing up." He drank deeply from his smoothie cup. "And it wasn't your fault. You didn't wield the blade that killed him."

She lowered her voice to a whisper. "That assassin was there for us, so it *was* our fault. After Dad died, Alex and I swore to each other that we would take care of you."

"And you have," he said. "But now I'm an adult. I'm fine. I can take care of myself. You need to live your own lives. And you need to let me live mine."

The phone in Sera's pocket buzzed. She snuck a peek at the number and saw that it was Kai. Again. What was that, like the fourth time today? She stuffed it back into her shorts. They'd planned to meet after lunch, and she saw no reason to speak to him a second earlier. In fact, she had about four-million-and-two reasons not to.

"Are you going to get that?" Riley asked.

"No."

"Avoiding someone?"

"Yes."

He snickered. Sera thought about telling him she was avoiding his psychopath of a new friend, but decided against it. She wanted to keep him as far away from all of this as she possibly could.

"Here's the thing, Riley. I do realize I've been very protective of you. But it's only because I want you to be safe. If anyone found out about me and Alex, they might use you to get to us."

"Ifs and maybes," he replied. "Our world is a dangerous one, drenched in magic. And the humans are in many ways even more dangerous. I or you or Alex might be killed at any time. That's precisely why we need to live, not hide."

The magic around them shifted up a gear. The breeze died, and the cool air suddenly got very hot. Sera looked past Riley, spotting the cause of the shift right away. Two mages were crossing the parking lot. Flames licked their hands. All four eyes were fixed on her, promises of pain etched in them.

"Hold that thought," she told Riley.

Then she stepped out to meet them, wondering why

113

she couldn't go a single day without being attacked by some idiot or another.

CHAPTER FIFTEEN
Fire

SERA HADN'T BROUGHT along her sword. She never carried it while running, though the sight of someone running with a sword strapped to her back was not an uncommon sight on the streets of San Francisco. That was only one of many strange sights you witnessed daily when you lived in one of the world's supernatural hotspots.

Sera *had* brought along a pair of knives. She drew them from the straps around her thighs, wondering how much good they'd do against the pair of fire-happy mages. The flames on their hands spread up their arms. Their skin glowed like orange embers, and golden lights danced in their eyes. A funnel of fire exploded from one of the mages' fingertips, blasting toward her like a stampede of burning horses. She darted away, but it followed. Trashcans crashed and car alarms blared as she tried to circle around the mages. A fire ball flew over her head.

"Hey, now that was just *rude*," she told the second mage. The faint scent of burnt hair filled her nose. She patted down her ponytail to make sure it wasn't on fire.

He threw back his head and cackled. Yeah, that's right.

He apparently fancied himself a cartoon character. There was an eerie and now familiar gleam in his eyes, just like Finn, Olivia, and all of the other psycho mages she'd fought over the past several days. Every single one of them seemed to be auditioning hard for Magic Junkie of the Year.

Mr. Funnel's fire hose had gone dry. Sustained streams of magic were hard work to keep up. They drained even veteran mages pretty fast, and these two were as green as the first grass in springtime. It was as though someone had suddenly pumped them full of magic they had no experience handling. They were brash, foolish, and utterly drunk on magic.

Sera threw her knife through Mr. Funnel's foot, stapling it to the muddy ground. He squealed, the fire dying in his eyes, and she swung out her fist, clocking him in the head. He collapsed into a napping heap at her feet.

Another fireball flew at her. She dodged, but it passed too close too fast, gracing her skin. She bit down on her lips, sealing the pain inside. It wouldn't do her any good out in the open. Inside of her, she could channel it into fuel for her fight.

"You're fast," Fireball said.

He hurled fire at the tree beside her, and the canopy burst into flames. Burning leaves fell gently—almost peacefully—from the branches like soft snow. Sera ran out into the parking lot before any of them could fall on her.

"But not fast enough."

He fired another blast. She jumped back as a sizable chunk of asphalt cracked beneath her feet.

"Fire is light. Fire is might. It gives you power. It makes them—"

Steam and lightning exploded in a colorful ball around him. When the pink and blue lights had fizzled out and the steam had dissipated, Fireball was lying on the ground. Sera whipped around to find Riley standing at the edge of the parking lot, a translucent orb in his hand. She rushed over to him and swung her arm over his shoulder, leading him away.

"What did you do?" she asked in a harsh whisper, her head pressed close to his.

"A magic bomb. I've been developing them in my spare time."

"I had everything under control. And you are risking exposure."

"Uh, Sera. Just look around. We're pretty well exposed already."

She followed his gaze to the crowd of people who'd gathered all the way from the smoothie bar to the parking lot. They were gaping at the unconscious mages strewn across the asphalt battlefield—but more than that, they were gaping at her and Riley. A few of them had pulled out their phones and were taking videos. Some others were rapidly texting. Fantastic.

"Any hope of discretion died the second those mages charged across the parking lot with flaming hands," he continued.

"You're probably right." Sighing, she took out her phone and dialed Mayhem.

Fred answered on the second ring. "Hey, Sera, what's up?"

"Where's Fiona?"

"Ladies' room. She left me in charge," he said, clearly excited. Sera could picture him puffing out his chest with pride. "What can I do for you?"

"I have two bodies here at Smoothie Elixir in the Presidio."

There was a pause. All joy had died in Fred's voice when he spoke again. "Dead or alive?"

"Alive. They're unconscious. So I need the Extraction Team, not Disposal," she said. "Two elemental mages, early twenties and pretty high on magic. They seem to favor fire, so tell the team to wear fire-retardant gear."

"Ok." His voice cracked.

"Fred?"

"Yes?"

"Do it now, please. And tell them to hurry. The mages could wake up at any moment."

"Ok, Sera."

She hung up, then looked at Riley. "You stay here."

"Where are you going?"

"It will take the Extraction Team at least five minutes to get here. Probably ten." She took two decorative ropes off the side of the smoothie building. "In the meantime, I'm going to see what I can find to restrain our friendly fire mages."

CHAPTER SIXTEEN

Pier 39

"WHAT HAPPENED TO you at Smoothie Elixir this morning?"

Sera looked across the table at Naomi. The noonday sun shone down on her, making her silver hair sparkle like the ribbons that streamed from the handlebars of a child's bike. Behind her, bands of tourists flooded the passages of Pier 39, and cross-legged hippies sat smoking magic weeds. A light breeze slid off the bay, cool and salty.

"When you asked me to meet you here for lunch, I hadn't expected an interrogation," Sera replied.

"When I asked you to meet me here for lunch, you hadn't yet been attacked by a duo of fire-hurling mages. Is it true one of them kept up a fire stream for a good two minutes?"

"It sounds like you already know everything."

"Not everything. The attack was on the news in the Mayhem rec room."

Sera swore under her breath.

"The details were sketchy—and probably played up by the media."

Probably. The media was always all over supernatural events, but they cared more for the wow factor of magic than the hard, cold facts.

"So, what happened?"

"Riley and I went out for a run. We stopped for smoothies, and those bozos just attacked us." Sera tore a corner off her sourdough bowl and dunked it into her soup. "But if you were at Mayhem today, you must have seen the Extraction Team bring in the mages."

"They didn't bring them in."

The bread slipped from Sera's fingers. "What? I waited at the scene for them to come. I saw them load those mages into the truck as Riley and I left."

"Before they drove off, some fancy lawyer arrived," Naomi told her. "She works for one of the big magic dynasties."

"Which one?"

"Sage."

Go figure.

"Anyway, she had some papers signed by the Magic Council stating that the Sage Dynasty was taking responsibility for the delinquents, and they would deal with their punishment. Our team had no choice but to hand them over."

So Harrison Sage had sent the fire mages to…to do what? To silence Sera? He hadn't spoken one word to her last night, and yet he'd somehow come to believe that she knew something that threatened him. Maybe he'd had her and Kai followed. Maybe he knew they were working together. Well, if he'd sent people to deal with her, he was worried. And only people who were up to something had a reason to be that worried.

But none of that bothered her like the mention of the

Magic Council had. Were they a part of this too, or had they just blindly signed off on one of Harrison Sage's projects? Kai had said that Harrison was on the Council.

"Does this attack have anything to do with your job for Drachenburg?" Naomi asked her.

"How do you know about that? Simmons never spills the details of the big cases. He thinks that gives them an air of mystique—and us the drive to strive to be better so we can land them."

"Yeah, that's what he says, but it's all talk. He pays well, but not well enough to stop gossip," said Naomi. "Sera, *everybody* at Mayhem knows about your big case. Especially Roberts. Cutler also, but I think he's more jealous of Drachenburg than of you. He's been going around telling everyone that you and he are going to celebrate at Liquid when you're done with the case."

"In his dreams."

"Cutler's kind of on his own plane." Naomi's eyes drifted off for a moment before she steered her gaze back to Sera. "So does this have to do with your job for Drachenburg or not?"

"Maybe. Or maybe I just pissed off someone who likes to hold a grudge. We've put away a lot of supernatural delinquents."

"You could have asked the fire mages what they wanted."

"I was pretty busy dodging fireballs, but next time I'll be sure to make time for smalltalk," Sera said drily.

Naomi chuckled, and her hair went blue. "How is your assignment going?"

"Well, in the last twenty-four hours, I've been attacked by telekinetics and elementals, teleported across the Golden Gate Bridge, had the backs of my legs turned into ground beef—"

"The Hello Kitty bandages look great, by the way."

"Thanks." Sera tore another piece off her bread bowl and ate it.

"The Drachenburgs are like the most famous magic dynasty—anywhere. What's it like working with one of them?"

"You don't work with a Drachenburg. You work *for* them. Kai is an arrogant, self-entitled control freak with enough destructive magic spilling out of him to bring on an eternal winter."

Naomi folded her hands up into a tent and balanced her chin on them. "Oh, Kai, is he? So what did you and *Kai* do yesterday?"

Sera did her best to ignore the smirk on Naomi's face. "We went to Magical Research Laboratories and did a little replay of our fight on Wednesday. It turns out Mr. Crazy Pants Mage is his cousin."

"Hmm."

Sera told her about the glyphs, and how she and Kai were shoved through them during the fight with Olivia and the other mages.

"I've heard of those glyphs. Fairies used to use them too."

"Do you know how to activate them? One of the mages did it during the fight, but when Kai tried later, nothing happened, no matter what magic he threw at them."

"My grandma once told me that the key to activating the glyphs was not to attack them, but to feed them some of your magic."

"What's their teleporting range?"

"It's dependent on the power level of the mage or fairy performing the magic."

"Interesting. Thanks."

"No problem." She smiled. "So then what happened?"

"By the time we got back to MRL, the mages were gone. And they'd stolen something from the vault. Ever heard of Priming Bangles?"

Naomi shook her head, her blue locks bouncing off her cheekbones. "Sorry, no."

"After that, we drove to Illusion."

"The super-fancy, super-exclusive, top-tier-mages-only restaurant in the Presidio?"

"Uh, yeah."

Naomi snickered.

"What?"

"Kai Drachenburg took you on a date."

Sera shot her an annoyed look.

"This is wild."

"This isn't wild. And it wasn't a date," Sera argued. "We were working."

"Interrogating the gold-plated forks, I'm sure."

"No, interrogating Harrison Sage."

Naomi's platinum eyebrows lifted. "And before that?"

"Before that, we ate. But it was only because we were so hungry from fighting all those mages," she added quickly.

"Yeah, hunger is typically why people eat. What did you have?"

"Steak."

Her brows slid higher. "Steak at Illusion is like a month's paycheck. I hope it was good."

"It didn't cost that much, it was good, and Kai paid anyway."

"Date," Naomi's lips popped.

"Work expense."

"You keep telling yourself that, Sera." She blinked, and

when she opened her eyes again, they were hazel.

"Wow, you're getting good at that. All your practice is really paying off."

"Thanks." She grinned. "And stop changing the subject. What happened after dinner?"

"Kai drove me home."

"And then?"

"And then nothing."

Naomi's grin widened, showing off her perfect white teeth. They were flat and beautiful, not pointed and scary like some types of fairies. "You're not a very good liar, fyi. You get really still whenever you're trying to hide something."

"Thanks for the tip."

"You're welcome. Now you can repay me by spilling the beans."

"He drove me home."

Naomi nodded.

"He walked me to my door."

She leaned in.

"And then…and then he kissed me."

The surprise flashed first across her face, but the delight stayed longer. "Oh, yes, my dear, that was a date."

Sera couldn't think of a clever retort, so she kept her mouth shut.

"A date with Kai Drachenburg!" Her hands buzzed with excitement. "Not that I blame you for going out with him. Did you see him on the cover of Mages Illustrated?"

"No."

"He was topless."

Sera rolled her eyes.

"And flexing." Naomi began to fan herself.

"Stop that."

"He is one gorgeous man, Sera."

"He's manipulative and arrogant."

"Of course he is. Just look at who his family is: the prestigious Drachenburg Dynasty. They own the world's largest consortium of magic companies. They have a seat on the Magic Council."

"And who sits in that seat?"

"Your new boyfriend."

Sera went hot and cold, all at once. "He's not my boyfriend," she managed to ground out—barely. Her jaw was stuck.

Naomi ignored her protest. "You didn't know he was on the council?"

Sera shook her head. That part of her body was still working. For now. She stirred whirlpools in her soup with her spoon.

Kai was on the Magic Council. Well, of course he was. Deep down, she'd known it all along but refused to admit it to herself. And all because she was attracted to him. Stupid, stupid, stupid.

This ended now. Things could never work out for them, even assuming he wasn't stringing her along for kicks, which she wasn't all that convinced of. The fact of the matter was, he was on the Magic Council, and she was the abomination the Magic Council had sentenced to death. That sort of relationship was as doomed as an ice sculpture in the desert.

She ate her lunch in silence, promising herself that she wouldn't let him kiss her again. When he kissed her, she lost all sense. In fact, she needed to figure out a way to block out his magic asap because it was just as bad. It felt so good that she didn't even care that the sweet song it sang was all a big, fat lie.

"What are you thinking about, Sera?" Naomi asked her.

About Kai naked. About sliding her hands over his hard abs. Wait, no. Not about that. Nothing about him. She kept quiet.

Naomi's young, wise eyes met hers. "You're thinking about Kai Drachenburg, aren't you?"

"Yes."

"Good."

Sera didn't turn when the familiar voice spoke. Not right away. And when she finally did, she wished she hadn't. Kai stood behind her chair, looking as good as ever in his signature fitted t-shirt and rugged jeans, his hair just messy enough to make him look relaxed but not sloppy. As she met his gaze, his magic—which he'd coiled so tightly around himself that she hadn't even sensed his presence— flared out, hitting her like a shockwave. Naomi let out a soft gasp.

"I've been trying to reach you all day, Sera. You'd better have a damn good reason for ignoring my calls," the dragon said.

CHAPTER SEVENTEEN

The Mystic Palace

HE'D FOUND HER. Somehow. Sera gave him a hard, long stare, all the while wondering how much he'd overheard.

"Sera, we have to move. I've had a lead on the case."

"Ok." She set some money on the table, then pushed back her chair. "See you later, Naomi."

Naomi bobbed her head, her gaze still locked on Kai. Maybe she'd never seen a dragon before. Kai just marched off, leaving Sera scrambling to catch up. They walked in silence along the water, passing docks, restaurants, and boatloads of tourists. On one of the water platforms, a herd of selkies were bathing in the sun. They were one of the area's biggest tourist attractions, and sure enough, a crowd stood nearby, clicking photos with their cameras.

"I tried calling you," Kai finally said, his words as hard as granite. "Multiple times."

"I know. I was ignoring you."

He stopped suddenly and spun around to face her. "You will tell me why."

"No." She crossed her arms and stared back. "I won't."

"Woman, you must have a death wish. No one can be this foolish."

"We've discussed this before. I'm a dumb brute who runs after monsters."

"So you say."

"How did you even find me?" she asked. "Did you have someone track my phone or something?"

"After I heard about the attack on you this morning, I tried calling you again."

"Ah, you were worried. How cute."

Smoke started rising from his hair.

"Nice trick. Did they teach you that in your fancy pants mage school?"

"When you didn't respond," he continued, every word crisp and tightly controlled, like he was on the brink of losing his cool. Maybe poking the dragon hadn't been such a good idea after all. "I decided to look for you. But I didn't need to track your phone. As soon as I went looking, I could feel your magic from clear across the city."

He towered over her, his body blocking out everything. There was nowhere else to look. She saw only him. He leaned down, his cheek brushing against hers. His skin was smooth and smelled of magic and masculine spice. So this is what dragons smelled like. She inhaled deeply, letting it soak into her.

"Your magic is intoxicating, Sera." His words buzzed against her skin. "So delicious, like a slice of dark chocolate cake."

She remembered last night—and how good it had felt to kiss him. She sensed her body leaning toward his, yearning for another taste.

"Did you like the cheesecake I left you?"

"I didn't eat it." She fought the urge to touch him.

"Riley did."

He laughed under his breath. "Stubborn woman, it was meant for you. I could see you wanted it. Why do you always insist on denying yourself what you want?"

"I don't—"

"Like your magic." He traced his finger down her arm, trailing invisible fire across her skin. "You hide it away when all it wants is to be free. I want to see what you can do when you really let it out."

Then he pulled away, leaving her breathless. She backed up and bumped against the metal railing. Nearby, the selkies raised their voices, singing out in seal-like barks.

"You should see your face," he said, watching her with smug eyes.

Jerk. He was playing games with her. And she'd let herself be played. It might be too late to save face, but she sure as hell was going to try.

"Did Dawson finish going through the vault?" she asked, steering the conversation back to work.

His face shifted gears. "Nothing else was taken."

"So the thieves' target was the Priming Bangles."

"Apparently."

"I've learned some more about the glyphs," she said.

"Tell me."

"Naomi told me how to activate them," Sera said, trying to speak over the selkies, who were getting louder with every passing second. She stole a glance back at the herd; two of them were fighting over a gem-studded comb, while the others cheered them on. "Hitting the glyphs with offensive magic doesn't work. You need to pour some of your magic into them."

"Interesting. Like jumpstarting a car battery."

"Yeah, kind of like that. The more magic you can pour

into it, the further you can teleport."

"Good to know." He walked across the path to a black car parked between two very large flower pots.

"Is this your car?"

The headlights blinked. *Well, I guess that answers that question.*

"That's not a parking spot," she told him.

He held open the door for her. "Really? The car seems to fit just fine."

"That's not the point. You're illegally parked."

"Everything else was full," he said with a shrug. "And the only reason I had to come here in the first place is because you weren't answering my calls."

"So it's my fault then?"

"No, it's no one's fault because there is no fault. My car fit here, so I took the spot."

"And if it hadn't fit here? If you'd driven the tank?"

"The tank?"

"Your big black car from yesterday," she said. "So if your car hadn't fit, would you have just parked here anyway, smashing the flower pots into tiny little pieces?"

"We're facing a major threat to the city, and you're worried about a couple of flower pots? You really have your priorities mixed up." He pointed into the car. "Get in. We have to hurry."

Thus told off, she sat down and pulled the door shut after her. Kai had a point, but so did she.

"You can't just do whatever you want," she told him as he started the engine.

The car roared across the pavement, scaring seagulls and scattering tourists. It shot out onto the street and squeezed between two cars. Brakes screeched, horns blared, and two angry—and completely freaked out—drivers shot him rude hand gestures.

"You did that to prove a point," she said.

"I don't need to prove anything." He sped up, and the engine purred in appreciation. "Now tell me about the mages who attacked you this morning."

Sera gritted her teeth at the order but told him anyway. She needed to see what he made of Harrison Sage's part in it and the Magic Council's interference. After all, he knew them all a whole lot better than she did.

"So Harrison sent one of his lawyers," he said when she was done.

"That means he's involved."

"Not necessarily. But likely."

"Maybe he sent the mages after me."

"Maybe."

"The Magic Council signed off on this. They gave him the authority he needed to waltz in and whisk the mages away. Do you know anything about that?" she asked him.

"Why would I?" He looked surprised. Then again, he was a manipulative beast. There was a reason dragons were often the villains of the story.

"Why would you? Because you sit on the Council," she shot back. "Which you failed to mention, by the way."

"Do you mention everything about yourself? No, you have it all tucked away in protective wrap like a snowball in July. And just like that summertime snowball, you cannot escape your fate."

Sera went cold. Her fate. If the Magic Council got its way, that meant death.

"Look, I don't care that you think you have weird magic, and I don't care why you're hiding it. People have all kinds of crazy reasons for doing foolish things, and I'm not going to try to stop you from being crazy or foolish. I don't even think that's possible." He sighed. "So be crazy and foolish and whatever else you want. But I've tasted your magic. I *will* find out what it is. And when I do, I'll be keeping you and your magic all to myself."

The possessiveness in his voice almost earned him a well-deserved punch to the face. But he was driving, so that would be stupid. And the need in his eyes threw her for a loop. And the way he was angled toward her...like he meant to protect her. She definitely believed him when he said he wouldn't tell anyone.

Games. More games, a voice said inside her head.

Right, she agreed, even as she realized that only crazy people heard voices in their heads.

The voice spoke again, *Don't trust anyone. You can protect yourself. Just like it's always been.*

Yeah, she'd taken care of herself, but her life had pretty much sucked up to now. Riley was right. This was no way to live. Sera didn't point that out to the voice. Arguing with the voices in your head was even crazier than hearing them.

"Kai—"

"I've said all that I mean to on this matter for now, Sera. If you still want to pretend to be offended, we can discuss that after we're done saving the city from the League of Mad Mages."

He was right. Work first.

"Why did the Magic Council give Harrison the authority to deal with those two mages?" she asked him.

"I don't know. I haven't met with them since I started working on this case. I didn't even know they'd met. I sure wasn't told about it. Harrison must be behind this," he said. "Well, I'll just ask him when we find him."

"Is that where we're going now? Is that the lead you mentioned?"

"Yes, my people have been trailing Harrison. They followed him to Acceleration Magic."

"The indoor recreational area near the Palace of Fine Arts?"

"Yes. Have you been there?"

"I corralled a herd of unicorns into there once."

His gaze flicked briefly to her before returning to the road. "How do you even corral a herd of unicorns?"

"With much difficulty," she told him. "So Acceleration Magic. That's where you're taking us?"

"Yes. Harrison went into the building a few hours ago and hasn't come out since."

"Did you mention that he's probably linked to a group of mages who can use glyphs to teleport across the city?"

"Yes, and they're keeping an eye on him and the others inside. Olivia showed up half an hour ago. Something big is brewing."

"Then let's get there before it explodes."

A few minutes later, Kai's car slid into a parking spot just outside of Acceleration Magic. The curved shell building that held the recreation area was drab, ugly, and uninspired—a complete contrast to the beautiful curves and colors of the nearby Palace of Fine Arts.

The fairies called the architectural landmark the Mystic Palace. On dark, clear nights you could sometimes watch them gathering to sing under the hollow palace dome, or see nymphs splashing in the pond. It was best to watch from a distance, however, because the fairies didn't take kindly to invaders of their rituals. The nymphs, on the other hand, delighted in the sight of visitors. They pouted out their lips, perked up their peaches, and shot sultry looks at any man within flirting distance. The men they lured in woke up the next morning with no memory of the previous night—and sometimes the past few days. But still the men kept coming, drawn in by the nymphs' seductive magic.

"My team's on the roof," Kai said, stopping in front of the building. His eyes panned up the smooth wall.

"I take it there's no ladder."

"No." He headed for a tree growing beside the building. It reached higher than the roof, but the branches were spaced too far apart to comfortably climb it. "We go up here."

The branches apparently weren't too far apart for a big, bad dragon—though she wasn't convinced those skinny twigs could even hold his weight. Maybe he meant to fly up.

"Do you want a boost?" he asked, his brows lifted in wicked amusement.

That'd be the day. "I'm fine."

She backed up to the grassy patch past the parking spaces. Then, taking a deep breath, she made a dash for the building, running up the wall to launch herself into the tree. Her foot slipped against one end of the branch, her hands locked onto the other, and the rest of her in between just tried to steady itself before she dropped to the ground like a stone. A few undignified squirms and wiggles later, she was making her way up the tree.

As she slid up onto the roof, she peeked down over the edge. Kai hopped onto the tree and scrambled up it like he did that sort of thing every day. Maybe he did. Who knew what sort of weird things he had in his dungeon—uh, basement.

In the middle of the roof, surrounding a skylight, three men dressed in full bodysuits turned their hard, assessing eyes on her. Their hands slid toward their knives.

"Stand down," Kai told them as he pushed himself up onto the roof.

His arms bulged under the weight. Not that Sera was ogling. Not at all. He winked at her on his way over to join his team of unsuitably dressed commandos. They must have been sweating up a storm under all that black.

"Sera, this is Callum, Tony, and Dal."

They each gave her a crisp nod.

"There are five mages inside," one of the men reported. "Three are piling up wood in the corner. And the two Sage siblings are arguing over something."

"What kind of wood?" Sera asked, crawling forward to peer through the skylight. The glass was too milky to see a thing. She looked at him in surprise.

"Tony's a seer," Kai told her.

She looked at Tony. "What's your range?"

"About thirty feet," he replied. "And the wood's oak."

"That's used for protection magic," said Sera. "What are those mages doing in there?"

"I don't know. But one of them just brought in the Priming Bangles," he said, looking at Kai.

"Ok, we're moving in."

Like perfect soldiers, they moved quickly into position. Sera wasn't a perfect soldier, and she didn't have a position —at least not any that he'd given her.

"What do you want me to do?" she asked Kai.

"We're all going to jump down."

"Without ropes?"

"I'll create a wind funnel to soften our landing. I'll use a second one to hold the mages in place," he said. "We'll recover the Priming Bangles and capture Harrison's rogue band of mages."

Kai hit the skylight with a blast that sucked it right out

of its screws. As the sheet of glass tumbled off the roof, the wind funnel poured through the opening.

"Sounds simple enough," she said cautiously.

Except that nothing was ever that simple.

CHAPTER EIGHTEEN

War with the Wind

IT TOOK A special sort of subtlety and a hell of a lot of power to tame a tornado. Kai had both in spades. As the tornado he'd cast began to spin into existence, he reached out and molded it into a slide. Sera, Kai, and the commandos rode the wind down to the ground, where a whirling funnel had the five mages pinned against the walls: Harrison and Olivia Sage, an elemental, a summoner, and a shifter. The elemental's magic smelled like fire, the summoner's like the sea, and the shifter's like a woodland. Harrison and Olivia smelled like old magic and self-entitlement mixed with blood and decay. Ew. They all smelled like a whole lot of crazy.

The fiery elemental tried to summon a ball of fire into her hand, but the wind puffed it out like a birthday candle. She tried again, and a wind tentacle curled out to slam her wrist against the bare concrete wall behind her. Glass crunched, likely from her expensive watch.

Harrison Sage glared out through the wind curtain, his hands tugging against the wall of magic. His malachite-green eyes gleamed with that now familiar manic energy.

Beside him, Olivia's eyes glowed like boiling honey. More mage zombie puppets for Team Apocalypse. But where was the puppet master? And how had he managed to place two first tier mages under his spell?

"You cannot break free," Kai said, watching Harrison's war with the wind.

Harrison's malachite eyes began to pulse with sick, nauseating magic. They looked like a pair of lightbulbs with a loose connection.

"Creepy," Tony commented, and the other two commandos nodded in agreement.

A translucent, semi-solid glob of magic oozed out of Harrison's hand, slid down his leg, and rolled across the floor onto the array of glyphs. There it dissolved, letting off a whiff of lemon-scented magic as it melted into the arcane symbols. In unison, Harrison and Olivia swung out their fists to punch through the wind barrier. The punch didn't shatter the whole thing—Kai's magic was too strong for that—but it did tear a sizable hole in it. Before Kai could seal the gap, the Sage siblings jumped through the glowing glyphs and disappeared. The portal snapped shut with a heavy pop, sucking all the magic out of the room.

Free of their tornado prison, the remaining three mages stepped forward with demented grins. Flames burst to life in the elemental's hands, singeing the cuffs of her jacket. She was dressed in a black skirt suit that belonged in some fancy New York City high-rise office, not a dusty, dirty storage room. She was wearing high-heeled pumps, for heaven's sake. Battle wear it was not.

On either side of her, the summoner and the shifter unrolled their power. Ribbons of glowing magic swirled up from the summoner, spitting out a swarm of seagulls that swerved and spun overhead like a bunch of bats out of a horror movie. Muscle rippled across the shifter's body. A low, deep growl rumbled deep in his chest. A werewolf. Shit.

"We don't have time for this," Kai said, growling back.

Most mages who could change shape took at least a minute to shift. This one had only half-morphed into a werewolf when Kai exploded into a dragon. And an explosion it truly was. One moment he was a man and the next…he was something very inhuman. Dragon Kai was well over twenty feet tall, so enormous that his shift had taken down a sizable chunk of the roof. He was as black as pitch with a dark blue-green sheen to his scales and wings, like a dragonfly. His eyes were that same devastatingly beautiful shade of electric blue.

The flock of seagulls turned into a steep dive, angling for Sera. The dragon snapped out his jaws, swallowing them up in a single bite. As the summoner fainted, the elemental shot a fireball at Kai. It bounced off his scales with a melodic clink. Rolling his enormous eyes, the dragon smacked her against the wall. She didn't get up. Now alone, the werewolf stared up at the prime predator, his eyes growing wide. Then he turned and made a run for it.

He wasn't fast enough.

The dragon raised his foot, lethal yet still somehow elegant, and stomped down on the fleeing werewolf. Yelp. Crunch. Holy shit.

Magic snapped, unwinding the layers of dragon until Kai was a man again—well, in the shape of a man again. The dragon was still lurking inside of him. That dragon stared out at her from behind magic-charged eyes.

"What the hell is the matter with you?" Sera demanded.

He blinked, apparently surprised. Maybe no one had ever dared to tell off the big, bad dragon before.

"He was retreating," she pushed on. "You did the equivalent of shooting him in the back." *But with a crunch.* She cringed.

"You kill monsters for a living. Don't tell me you've suddenly decided to be squeamish," he said, disapproval in his voice.

"It's not the same at all. That was a man, not a beast. And you are a psychopath."

Kai shrugged. "He's not dead." His eyes flicked over to the broken body she was making a concentrated effort not to see. "He turns into a werewolf. He'll heal."

"And you turn into a dragon. So it's ok if I poke you with my sword?"

Kai flashed his teeth at her. "You're welcome to try, sweetheart."

She rolled her eyes. Dragons. "Whatever. We can duel it out in your dungeon later."

Magic flickered in his eyes.

"Uh, that didn't come out right." She cleared her throat. "Let's just concentrate on our more immediate problem. Harrison and Olivia got away. *With* the Priming Bangles."

"I can feel them." His lids dropped. "They're close. But where?" He grabbed a hold of her hand.

"What do you think you're doing?"

"Shh," he said, taking her other hand. His magic poured through their joined hands, pulsing through her body. "I need you, Sera."

Her breath caught in her throat.

"...to help me find them," he continued. "If we combine our magic, it will be easier to track them down."

"But—"

"No buts. The men won't say a thing about your magic." He opened his eyes to look at the trio of commandos.

"Nope."

"Not a word."

"Our lips are sealed."

"There you go," said Kai.

It wasn't the commandos she was worried about. She believed them when they said they wouldn't snitch; the look in their eyes said they'd follow Kai's orders to their graves. No, they weren't the problem. The problem was Kai. Kai the dragon. Kai the insanely powerful mage who sat on the Magic Council. He was the one she had to worry about. He just didn't know it yet.

"Now for once don't be stubborn," he said. "This is about more than just you. Someone is taking control of the city's mages. I don't have to tell you how bad it will be if he turns his new army against the other supernaturals—or the humans. Remember what Finn saw."

He was right. Damn him. If this mess tore the city apart—or worse yet, spread even further—she'd have bigger problems than her own life. Thousands could die. Or even millions. She couldn't let the whole world go to hell just to save herself. If she did that, she'd be no better than those who had sentenced her kind to death. Steeling herself, she nodded at Kai.

"Good." His hands slipped out of hers. "Here, I'll help you." He slid them up her arms with languid relish, finally settling them on her shoulders. "Reach out with your magic and try to find mine."

A million voices began to scream warnings in her head. *Dragon! Danger! Magic Council! Death!* She pushed them down, opening a hole in her shield just large enough to squeeze out a slender sliver of magic. She extended it toward him.

"Good," he said as her magic brushed against his. "Now we need to get our magics to merge."

"How do we do that?"

"By putting them on the same magical wavelength. Since you're new at this, I'll adjust to your magic."

His magic shifted to a higher note, humming against hers.

"Not quite right," he said.

It shifted up again. And again. He tried down. Then up again. Four more times he tried without success. Sweat beaded his hairline.

"Your magic's rhythm seems to elude me. Let's see if you have better luck." He took her hand and set it on his chest. "Magic is like blood. It pumps out from the heart. Get a feel for its rhythm and try to match it."

Beneath her hand, Kai's chest thumped with the power of a war hammer. His magic pulsed out, spreading up one arm and down the other, pouring through every pore in her body. She closed her eyes and opened her senses. Kai's magic sounded like the beating wings of a giant dragon. It smelled like burning timber, hot and sweet, and it tasted like cinnamon. It was the most beautifully devastating thing she'd ever experienced. She melted into blissful oblivion under its strong and subtle velvet touch.

"Sera?"

"Yes?" Her voice was deep and throaty.

"I think…oh, God, please, stop doing that."

For the first time since she'd met him, she could feel a weakness in his self-control. She slid her magic against the weak spot, trying to pop it open. A deep, primal growl rumbled inside his chest. The temptation to break through his control overwhelmed her.

"Sera." His fingers massaged her head through a curtain of long hair. Her ponytail had come loose, and she didn't care. "You're almost there."

"I know," she breathed, pushing her magic into alignment with his. As their magics locked together into one note, liquid heat flooded her body, driving out what little was left of rational thought. So this was what being drunk on magic felt like. For the first time, she understood how mages turned into magic junkies—and why they never wanted the rush of magic to end.

Kai's soft lips brushed up her neck. "Slap me."

"Why?"

He kissed her ear as he spoke. "Because you need to snap me out of your spell."

"Why?"

His mouth hovered over hers. "Because if you don't, I'll have no choice but to start doing things to you that you'll really, really enjoy."

She snorted.

"You don't believe me?" His hand slid over her bottom.

"No, I don't. Your men are watching."

"Is that your only problem? In that case." He kissed her cheek once, then turned his head to look at the three commandos. "Guys, turn around."

As one and without a word, they pivoted around, turning their backs to Sera and Kai.

"You're serious?"

He leaned in to kiss her long and deep—then pulled back, leaving her lips burning for more. "I'm serious and then some."

She drew a deep breath, struggling to steady her racing

heart. "I'm not going to have sex with you."

He arched an amused brow. "No?"

"No. And definitely not while the commando triad is here."

"Should I have them take a walk?" he said, the words lingering on his lips.

Yes. "No," she asserted, mentally slapping herself. "I've aligned my magic with yours. Now tell me what to do next."

He wet his lips.

"About finding the Sages, you crazy dragon."

Feather-light, his hand caressed her cheek.

She glared at him. "Do you want that slap now?"

"No, let's save that for later." There was something really indecent about the way he said it. "Ok, tracking. What's the furthest you've ever been able to track someone?"

She swallowed hard before answering. "The same room usually. Sometimes the same building."

"Nothing further?"

"No."

"You haven't been training your magic."

Sera stiffened. There it was again: disapproval. At least it put some ice on the fire.

"With your power level, I'm willing to bet you could even track someone with only trace amounts of magic from across the city," said Kai. "After a bit of training. We don't have time for that right now, so I'll just draw on your magic to boost my range."

The tendrils of their magic had intertwined into a lattice of tiny connections. Every single one of these connections began to tingle as Kai drank from her magic. His eyes, dilated from the magic influx, looked upward.

When he spoke, his voice was distant.

"They're moving along the waterfront. They have the Priming Bangles with them. I see large ferries crowded full of people…"

The band of magic connecting Sera to Kai snapped. His magic faded, leaving her cold and more than a little humiliated. Separated from the sensual caress of his magic, her head was finally clear enough to realize what a fool she'd made of herself. She'd teased him, tasted him, and wanted more. But she wasn't one to let a little thing like complete and utter humiliation stand in the way of her doing her job.

"Where are they going?" she asked Kai.

"Alcatraz," he said. "They're going to Alcatraz."

CHAPTER NINETEEN
Tanked Dragon

THEY ALL PILED into Kai's car, and he zoomed out of the parking lot like his tail was on fire. Maybe he'd set it on fire himself. Sera snickered from the passenger seat. Kai turned his head to give her a stern look.

"Hey, watch the road!" she shouted, gesturing frantically.

Kai slipped in between two cars, cutting it so close that they'd probably need a new paint job. From the back seat, the commandos let out a round of manly chortles.

"I'm stuck in a car with a bunch of raving lunatics," she muttered.

The comment only elicited more chortles. Kai shot them a hard glare, and they fell silent.

"There's no need for concern," he assured her.

"You drive like you're replaying a high-speed chase scene from some action blockbuster movie."

"I know precisely what I'm doing."

"And you do this, Mr. Action, without keeping your eyes on the road."

"You worry too much."

"I worry too much?" she repeated in disbelief. "Well, I'm sorry if I'm not a big, bad, indestructible dragon who *steps* on people who annoy him."

"He didn't annoy me. He was a threat that had to be neutralized. If I hadn't shifted into a dragon, that werewolf would have snapped your pretty hands right off."

"He could have tried. And tasted my steel."

"And you call me violent," he said, glancing over at her.

"Eyes."

Smirking, he returned his eyes to the road.

"There's a really big difference between making someone go splat and using your sword to defend yourself against a direct assault," she told him.

"Were those caterpillars launching a direct assault on you?"

"As a matter of fact, yes. I'll have you know that those caterpillars have some pretty nasty spit. Like burning acid nasty. They were using it to terrorize the human and supernatural populations of the city. And when I asked them to stop, they got really unpleasant."

"It must have been the sword with which you asked them to stop."

Sera ignored the commandos' snickering and replied cooly, "Let's just try to get to the pier without hitting any of the other cars on the road."

"I would never hit anyone."

So said the man who stepped on people. He did look pretty horrified, though. Maybe he only used his powers against monsters.

"That would scratch the paint on my car," he added. "I'd just summon some wind to nudge them aside instead."

Or maybe he used his power whenever it was convenient for him.

"He's just pulling your leg," Dal called from the back seat.

Sera turned around to look at him. He wasn't a small man by any measure. In fact, he was a big, beefy, muscle mass currently sitting with his knees nearly up to his chin, and the two men on either side of him weren't any smaller. The three of them looked really uncomfortable squished into the backseat of the car, but when Kai had told them to sit there, they hadn't even blinked.

"He pretends to be callous, but he's actually very reasonable. And he's always really careful not to damage anything," said Callum.

"The roof of Acceleration Magic," she reminded them. "Or should I say, what's left of the roof of Acceleration Magic?"

"A minor miscalculation while shifting, I'm sure," Tony said.

"That roof did look higher than it was," agreed Dal.

"He only breaks something less than half the time he shifts into a dragon."

"And aren't dragons near-sighted?"

"No, far-sighted. They have to be able to see their prey from way up high so they can swoop down on it and carry it off for lunch."

"Or barbecue it."

"Yeah, that too."

Kai shot them an irate look through the rearview mirror. "You three are *not* helping."

"Hey, at least we didn't mention the tank," Callum said.

Tony shook his head. "Well, now you did."

"What happened with the tank?" Sera asked. They were baiting her, and she knew it. But she found herself really curious.

"Oh, no. You don't want to know about the tank," said Tony.

Dal nodded in agreement. "You're not ready to hear about the tank."

"Cut the drama and just tell me, guys."

Callum stole a cautious look at Kai, and when his boss didn't forbid him from speaking about this tank or anything else, he dove right into the tale. "Did Kai ever tell you what he did in the German military?"

"He said he played with tanks."

Callum snorted. "That's one way to put it. Or they played with him. Suffice it to say, he never got to drive any of the tanks."

"Doesn't driving a tank require special training?" Sera said.

"Which they didn't want to give me," Kai told her.

"Why not?"

"They kept me pretty busy running simulations."

"Like war games and such?"

"Not exactly. They told me to shift into a dragon and then had the tanks shoot all kinds of weird shit at me."

Sera opened her mouth to say something, but it took a few seconds for words to come out. "What happened?"

He shrugged. "Not much. Most of it just kind of tickled."

"Tanks shot at you, and it 'just kind of tickled'?"

"Yes."

Wow. Dragons were supposed to be pretty resilient to most magic you could throw at them, but that was magic. And he was talking about ammunition shot out of a tank.

"They tried a few nastier things, and those hurt," he continued. "One of them really hurt, and I got upset."

"That sounds ominous."

"I knocked over one of the tanks, and it broke."

"Tanks don't just break. They're pretty everything-proof."

"Well, they're not dragon-proof. And most certainly not pissed-off-dragon-proof."

"Did anyone get hurt?" she asked.

"No, it was remote controlled. But the military wanted me to pay for the tank I broke."

"And did you?"

"Of course not. Do you have any idea how much a tank costs?"

"A lot?"

"Yes, a lot," he agreed. "And it was their fault the tank broke. The German and American militaries were working on this big project together. A project that involved shooting KE uranium core bullets at me in dragon form. If they hadn't gotten that stupid idea into their heads, I never would have broken a tank. Afterwards, they insisted I pay for the American tank I broke. I refused. There was talk of disciplinary action."

"What did you do?"

"I left. I'd grown pretty tired of their games. In the beginning, it was funny to watch bullets bounce off my scales. I was young and cocky and liked to show off. Well, the novelty quickly wore off, and I realized I had better things to do than be their research pet."

"Did they still try to make you pay for the tank?" she asked him.

"Yes. They sent my father a bill. He sent them his lawyer. After that, we didn't hear anything from them again."

"Hmm," said Sera. "So what does this have to do with driving a tank?"

"A few months later, I came home to find a tank parked on our lawn," Kai replied. "It looked familiar."

"It was the tank he'd broken," Dal told her.

Sera looked at Kai. "So your dad did pay for it after all?"

"Not exactly."

"Then what?"

"They gave it to him."

"For free?"

"In exchange for towing it off. It was blocking a good portion of one of the fields, and they couldn't get it out of the mud."

Sera snorted. "You knocked a tank into the mud?" It was almost as funny as it was blood-curdling scary. Kai knocked over tanks like they were little toy cars. "And how did your dad get it out?"

"He brought along a few dozen telekinetics. They lifted the tank out of the mud, then my father towed it away. He had it restored and gave it to me for my birthday."

"Your dad…gave you a *tank* for your birthday?"

"Yes."

"Why?"

"It was my parents' way of getting me to come visit them more often. They knew I'd always wanted to drive a tank, and they had plenty of space on their property for me to do that."

"That's… It's just crazy," Sera said.

"Is it?"

"Yes. It is. Most people get things like books or clothes or gift cards for their birthday. You got a freaking tank."

"I see." He seemed to mull that over for awhile. Or maybe he was just contemplating how best to squeeze between the minivan and the Mini in front of him. "Do you like gift cards?" he finally asked.

"Not really. You can't usually buy weapons with them. And they're so impersonal. I wouldn't say no to a gift card from Wizard House Pizza, though."

Chuckling, he spun the car into a tight u-turn that knocked Sera against the window. Oxygen fled her lungs like an escaped prisoner flying the coop. Fresh off the spin, the car slid past a pickup truck angling for the last parking spot in sight. To the chorus of angry honks, Sera, Kai, and the commandos jumped out of the car.

"There!" Tony shouted over the wind, pointing to the ferry peeling away from the pier.

Sera ran all out, darting between tourists. The wind beat at her face, salting her tongue and chilling her skin. Kai and his team matched her stride for stride.

They were too late.

The ferry was gone, too far away for them to make a jump for it. Without stopping, Kai changed directions, angling for a row of motorboats. He hopped into a bright yellow one, and the commandos followed. Sera slowed but did the same.

"Don't tell me you have a boat at every dock in the area," she said as the motorboat zoomed off.

"No, of course not. That would be excessive."

Yeah, and having a car in every garage in the city is not excessive?

"We're just borrowing it for a short while."

"How often do you just 'borrow' things? And how often do those things survive to be returned to their unsuspecting owner?"

"Usually. I'm very careful. I hardly ever break anything."

She gave him a hard look. "You broke a military tank.

And I don't think you can simply order this floating banana out of a catalogue."

The commandos snickered.

"Watch your angle," Kai chided Callum, who was driving the boat. "And hurry up. They're almost to the island." He turned toward Sera. "Let's worry about catching those remote-controlled mages for now. Later, we can deal with bribing owners of floating bananas."

Sera nodded. The tour boat had reached Alcatraz. She could feel Harrison and Olivia on the island. She could feel other mages too—a lot of them. And every single one of them had that same bizarre magic. The mage zombies had taken over Alcatraz.

CHAPTER TWENTY
Alcatraz

AS THEIR BOAT pulled up to the dock, passengers were still filing off the ferry. A monstrosity of a building loomed over them, its dirty concrete walls bleeding rust. There was not a mage in sight, crazy or otherwise.

"That way," Kai said, pointing up the hill at the old cell house.

Sera felt it too. The mages were gathering. There were so many of them. Dozens and dozens. Their mad magic sang out, broadcasting their location to every corner of the island, like a lighthouse in a storm. Finding them wouldn't be a problem. It's what would happen *after* they found them that Sera was worried about. Even a dragon couldn't handle that many mages at once.

"We need a plan," Sera told Kai as she jogged up the hill beside him.

"I always have a plan." There was something foreboding in those eyes.

"Turning into a dragon and stepping on them all is *not* a plan."

"Sure it is. In fact, it's a damn good plan."

"What if the ceiling is too low to shift into a dragon?"

"I'll shift into a smaller dragon," he said. "Or cast some other sort of magic. The Storm of the Four Elements is very effective against multiple targets."

Yeah, and effective at bringing down the ceiling on us, she thought. "Harrison and Olivia just got here, but I'll bet most of the mages have been here for awhile."

"How do you know?"

"They... Well, their..."

"You felt the stale magic at the docks, didn't you?"

"Yes." That single word scraped against her tongue like a razor. She'd spent two decades keeping her mouth shut about her magic, and now she was deciphering magic tracks with a member of the Magic Council. Had Dad still been alive, he'd have already told her off fifty times over in that cool, calm voice that was so much worse than shouting. She shouldn't even be hanging around Kai.

"There are a few magic trails, mostly between three and five hours old," he said.

"That's long enough for them to have set up some defenses. What if they've booby-trapped their gathering space with magic that goes boom when we enter?"

"I don't think they're expecting company. Harrison and Olivia were obviously trying something with the Priming Bangles when we cornered them and they ran off here to join the rest of their cult. Whatever they have planned, it's probably not ready."

"Cult? Is that what you think it is?"

"Mages spontaneously getting more powerful and acting completely out of character," he said. "It sure has the makings of a bizarre cult, don't you think?"

"I suppose." Sera had no experience dealing with supernatural cults, just that one magic-drunk mage and a whole lot of regular supernaturals who were more than enough trouble as it was. "But they could still have defenses in place."

"My team has a lot of experience dealing with magical defenses."

She glanced sidelong at him. "You have an answer for everything, don't you?"

"Of course," he said, and climbed over a 'Closed for Renovations' sign to enter the old cell house.

Sera followed, and as she entered a cell block, the three commandos passed in front of her and Kai, presumably to put their 'experience dealing with magical defenses' to good use. She looked up at the levels of cells that stretched across either side of the cavernous room. She felt at the same time both very small and very claustrophobic. Alcatraz had once been a prison for the nastiest sort of supernatural criminals. The bars in this cellblock were made of iron, which bounced and bent magic like a room full of mirrors. The magical vibrations were giving Sera a migraine.

"…in the basement," Kai was telling the others.

Purple and yellow spots danced in front of her eyes. Heavy, resounding beats tore through her ears. Her skin was hot and sticky with sweat, and her stomach churned like the water beneath a budding hurricane. She stumbled forward and threw up all of her lunch.

"Sera?" Kai reached out and caught her as she swayed.

She couldn't speak. She couldn't even stand. Her head felt like it was stuck inside of a trash compactor.

"Block it out," his deep voice said over the pounding beat.

"Don't…know…how…" she croaked. Her mouth burned with acid. Her whole body was burning.

"It's like masking your magic but in reverse. Push out

your wall and turn it inside out. Instead of bottling your magic in, you want to keep other magic out."

Sera could hardly follow him. The pain was too much. If the entire building collapsed on top of her, it wouldn't have hurt this much. She reached toward the walls. She didn't have any magic that could bring down walls, but that wouldn't stop her from trying. She'd pound it with her fists if need be. Anything to end the pain. Anything to be free.

"Sera."

Something locked onto her, something strong and horrible that wanted her to suffer. She punched and kicked with all her strength, but the steel trap remained immovable. She couldn't break out of it.

"Sera, stop," Kai's voice whispered in her ear.

"Hurts."

"I know," his voice said in soothing tones. "But you can make it stop."

She looked desperately at the wall—the wall that she couldn't reach.

"No, not like that. I know you want to keep your magic coiled up inside of you, but that's what's hurting you. You need to push it out to make a barrier that will block everything out. You can do this."

The voice sounded sincere, but dragons were liars. She tried again to break free. When that didn't work, she reached up to the hard arms crisscrossed over her chest and pulled down on them. An unexpected jolt of magic tore out of her fingers.

"Is that the best you can do?" the voice taunted.

She dug her fingernails into him and hit him with her magic again.

He grunted. "Was that supposed to hurt?"

Sweat slid down her face like burning rivers. She dug

deep for her magic, letting it flow to the surface. Her head was exploding in agony, but she fought against the pain. She wound up her magic and shot it into him, putting as much power as she could into it. It was the magical equivalent of kicking someone in the head.

Too bad dragons had freakishly hard heads.

"It tickles." He spit out something. Blood? "Like the wings of a butterfly."

Sera clenched her teeth, funneling all her magic into a single concentrated punch. He stumbled back, and because the stubborn bastard still hadn't let go, she went with him. As they fell, the cork that had plugged her magic for over twenty years popped out. Her magic cascaded out of her, filling her with ecstasy that swallowed the pain. She pushed hard against her magic, flipping it out. The sickening magic vibrations winked out. The aftershocks of her own magical release lingered, slowly fading out.

"Sera, are you all right?"

She peeled her face off the rock beneath her. Except it wasn't a rock. She was lying on top of Kai, and he looked as smug as a kitten who'd caught his first mouse—or a dragon who'd caught his first sheep. She scrambled away from him, landing on her butt. She was still too dizzy.

"What was that?" she asked, her voice hoarse. She looked away from the wall. With the pain gone, she couldn't believe she'd ever fantasized about smashing her head through it.

Kai pushed up to sit cross-legged opposite her. "That was all the magic in the room, bounced off the iron bars a million or so times. One of the first things a mage learns is how to block that out, for reasons you can now appreciate."

She looked at the three commandos, who were standing at the other end of the room, leaning against the wall, their backs to her. "And what's wrong with them?"

"They're recovering."

"From what?"

"From that wave of exquisite magic you released. It was…overwhelming."

"You don't look overwhelmed," she said.

"Of course I am." His eyes dilated with magic, he lifted his hand to her face and brushed it softly against her cheek. "Are you ready to continue?"

"Are you?" she shot back, not even knowing what possessed her to say it. The dragon sure had a way of getting under her skin like no one else could.

"No, but I'll manage." He leaned in and kissed her once on the lips, feather soft, before pulling back. "If you three are sorted, let's head into the basement."

"Sure thing, boss." Tony cleared his throat. "We're ready."

The other two nodded, then they all walked toward the staircase that led to the basement—or dungeon, as it very clearly was. Moss was slowly consuming the brick walls, turning them from a warm gold-red color to putrid green. A web of cracks spread across the length of the tunnel's floor. Flickering wall lamps hung between tall doors that looked like the moat gates of a castle. Nothing about the atmosphere was particularly welcoming, and Sera felt a new wave of claustrophobia rush through her.

"I don't like how this feels." She said it so quietly that she didn't expect anyone to hear.

Proving that a dragon's hearing was as keen as his magic, Kai replied, "They've invited in dark magic."

"Dark magic? Like a demon?" she whispered.

"I don't know. It's…old. And powerful. It could be anything ancient: an artifact, a spell, a demon."

"A dragon?"

"Perhaps. But if they'd found a real dragon, I think most of the city would know about it. Dragons aren't subtle creatures."

"Neither are mages who shift into them," she muttered under her breath.

Kai said nothing, but the subtle twitch at the corner of his mouth told her he'd heard surely enough.

They passed several rooms, some empty and some stocked with piles of wood. Oak, like at the Palace, and a lot of it. The mages were planning on brewing up some heavy duty protection magic. The question was why? What were they trying to protect?

"We're close. There." Kai pointed at the closed door at the end of the tunnel. "They're in that room."

Tony pressed his hand to the door. "I see eight mages."

"There should be dozens. Where are all the rest?" Sera asked.

Kai shook his head. "I don't know. But they can't be far away. Callum, come stand in front with me. The two of us are going to put up a wind barrier to shield us from whatever magic they try to throw at us."

As Callum moved beside him, Kai continued, "Dal, I need you to cast a protective net behind us, just in case some of their friends are hiding back there, ready to rush us."

With Dal in place, Kai hit the door with a blast that ripped it off its hinges and shot it into the room. Subtle he was not. It was no wonder he liked tanks.

The wind barrier roared to life as they stepped into the room. Behind them, a net of sparkling gold lights materialized. Sera didn't know what it was, but something told her it could take a whole lot of damage. They were as ready as they'd ever be to take on the mage zombie cult.

Except the mages didn't attack. They just stood there, their crazed eyes watching them with demented delight. And it was only when Sera tried to take her next step that she realized why.

Her foot wouldn't move. Around her, Kai and the commandos jerked, also stuck. Sera looked down, but what she saw wasn't tar, or quicksand, or even magic tar or magic quicksand. It was something a million times worse: glowing glyphs. She didn't even have a chance to kiss that dingy dungeon goodbye before she and the others were sucked up into darkness and spit out into another dingy room.

Sera fell forward, tripping over a pile of broken bricks, but at least she managed to stay on her feet this time. She realized how irrelevant that was the moment she got a good look at the room—and the army of mages before her. She reached back and drew her sword. She'd never taken on this many mages, especially not ones juiced up on some crazy mix of joo joo. But as Kai was so fond of mentioning, he could just turn into a dragon and step on them. The three commandos didn't strike her as lightweights either. Kai Drachenburg was not the sort of man to employ lightweights.

Sera looked back at Kai, knowing that he'd shoot her a confident smirk. But he wasn't smirking. He wasn't even standing. Kai and the three commandos were lying unconscious on the floor, and she was all that stood between them and the army of mad mages.

CHAPTER TWENTY-ONE
Immune

THE LINE OF mages parted, and Olivia the crazy telekinetic stepped through.

"Now, aren't you interesting," she said, looking Sera over. "Why aren't you napping?"

"I don't nap."

Olivia arched a perfect eyebrow. "Oh, no?"

"Nope, no naps," Sera told her. "I usually don't even go to bed before midnight. I'm firmly in the insomniac camp." She was spewing nonsense, but none of that mattered. She had to keep Olivia talking long enough to...

To what, Sera? So what if you're good with a sword. There are two dozen of them, and only one of you. Every single one of those mages is drunk on magic. You don't stand a chance.

Sera knew the voice in her head was right, but she ignored it anyway. She had to think of something. If she couldn't fight, maybe she could at least figure out a way to wake the others. Five to twenty weren't great odds, but it sounded a whole lot better than one to twenty.

"Insomniac, you say?" Olivia laughed. "More like a freak of nature. That sleeping spell was cast by seven first tier mages. It even works against smug mages who fancy themselves a dragon." She sneered down at Kai before returning her haughty gaze to Sera. "But not you. What are you?"

"Sera Dering, mercenary." Grinning, she pushed out her hand. "Nice to meet you."

Olivia turned up her pouty little nose. "What are you, retarded or something?"

"I have no magic, and I kill monsters for a living." Better to let them think she had no magic. After a lifetime of pretending just that, it was an easy act to play. "My intelligence has been questioned on occasion. And my sanity too."

"It's no wonder Kai has a thing for you. He's a deranged little dragon," said Harrison, stepping up beside his sister.

"She's a regular nutcase herself."

Harrison's eyes panned down Sera's legs. "I think she's rather cute actually."

"Please. Don't tell me you're chasing after Kai's leftovers." Olivia frowned. "Again." She swept out her hand.

The pile of bricks beneath Sera's feet tumbled down, and with all the grace of a tripped elephant, she landed hard on her butt. Above her, Olivia snickered.

"She's nothing special. A freak. And one who is in desperate need of a makeover." She looked down on Sera, distaste oozing out of her exfoliated pores and dripping off of her. "My dear girl, hasn't anyone ever told you that the ghetto look is out this year?"

Yeah, Olivia Sage really needed a punch to her pretty face. Sera was happy to deliver it, but not just yet. She'd never cared what stupid mean people thought of her, and she wasn't going to start now. But maybe she could use this to her advantage. Sera gave her torn, dirty clothes a mortified look and scooted away from the telekinetic princess.

"Are my clothes really so bad?"

A predatory gleam flashed in Olivia's eyes. She thought she had her. "Not if you're fashioning yourself to spend your life as a hobo. But why anyone would *choose* to spend their life in such idle, filthy laziness I cannot even imagine."

"Oh." Sera scooted back again. "Well, I was planning on buying some new shoes." Scoot, scoot. "After I get paid for this job." Scoot, scoot. She bumped against Kai. Bingo.

"I have a feeling you won't be getting paid, dear."

Sera stretched her hand back to touch Kai's arm. She could feel the thin film of foreign magic wrapped tightly across his skin. Whatever it was, it sure was potent. That must have been the seven-mage sleeping spell. Funny, it had bounced right off of her. She'd never been immune to magic before. Maybe it was a fluke, a side effect of her weird magic. Or was this because Kai had told her to turn her magic barrier inside out? Was she reflecting magic like the prison bars had done to her? If so, her shield wasn't affecting any of the mages in the room. She didn't see anyone keeled over in pain.

"Soon Kai won't be in any condition to pay you," continued Olivia.

Which meant they expected to either bankrupt him or kill him. Kai had too much money and magic to make either of those an easy feat.

"Hush, you've already said too much," Harrison scolded her.

"She won't be around to tattle."

"I don't know. She might still be useful."

"Useful as what? Planning to clean her up, put her in a lacy nightie, and use her as your bedroom battle maiden ornament?"

Harrison frowned at her. "Don't be crass."

As they were busy bickering, Sera slid her fingers along Kai's wrist, tugging on the magic layer. A corner came loose, and she grabbed onto it, slowly peeling the film away. She unraveled it strand by strand, piece by piece, until she could feel him start to wake up.

"Getting defensive of your new ornament, are you?"

"Why do you always have to be the center of attention, Olivia? Why?" Harrison demanded.

"This isn't about me."

"No, it's not. But you're trying to make it be."

One of Kai's eyes blinked open, meeting Sera's gaze. She gave his hand a squeeze, willing him to brush off the final remnants of the sleeping spell.

"Oh, I'm sorry if you can't seem to get Mom and Dad's attention, no matter what silly nerd award you win," Olivia said.

"They know they don't need to worry about me. They're too busy cleaning up after your messes anyway. It must be exhausting to be a nonstop, one-person train wreck for the tabloids."

Kai kept his eyes on Sera as a ring of fire flared to life around the mages. The Sage siblings just kept on bickering, completely unaware that they'd been cut off from their army.

"You're just jealous that you don't get to be in the newspaper."

"I'm on the Magic Council. I have no need to toss my panties at the media to get their attention."

"I never—"

"Don't even deny it. It made the front page of Supernatural Times."

A sly grin spread across Olivia's coral lips. "Oh, right." She shrugged. "What can I say? The reporter was hot."

"I can't believe you managed to get the Priming Bangles out of Kai's vault without making out with his guards."

Harrison turned, and his exasperation melted into cold fury when he saw his army trapped behind a wall of fire. He spun around to glare at Sera, and his mouth flopped open when he found Kai standing beside her.

"You're supposed to be asleep," Harrison told him.

"The bed you provided was uncomfortable." Kai looked at Sera. "Try to wake up the others." He turned back to Harrison. "You will tell me what you're planning."

"You don't give orders here, Kai."

Deep vibrations echoed beneath the ground, rumbling the floor under their feet.

Harrison folded his arms across his chest. "And you're not going to intimidate me."

Having freed Tony from the sleeping spell, Sera set to work on peeling it off of Dal. "Threaten to step on him," she told Kai. "That'll make him talk."

"I thought you didn't approve of stepping on people." His magic was freckled with amusement.

"For those two, I'm willing to make an exception. Especially her." Sera glared at Olivia. "She said I looked like a hobo. And called me a bedroom ornament."

"Why on earth would you do a thing like that?" Kai asked her.

Olivia shrugged. "I speak only truths. I can't be blamed if she doesn't like it."

"You're lucky she didn't hack your arm off with her sword," Kai told her.

"That brute?" She sneered at Sera. "She wouldn't even dare."

A tendril of fire snapped at Olivia's arm, making her squeal and hop away. Kai looked back at Sera.

"Hey, stop hijacking my fire."

Despite his reproving words, he sounded more intrigued than annoyed. Sera didn't have a clue how she'd done it. She'd had a cruel desire to crack a fiery whip at Olivia, and the flames had simply complied. She helped Callum up, then reeled in her magic again. Letting it out had been a very bad idea. Her magic had a will of its own. Now that it had played a bit, it didn't ever want to go back inside and hide.

"She's insane," Olivia whined, massaging her arm. "Kai, are you going to let her treat me like this?"

"You stole from me, and you want my sympathy?"

She pouted out her lips. "Yes. We're equals. The magical elite. We play. We fight. We make up." Olivia pointed her fake fingernail at Sera. It was a top-of-the-line fake fingernail, but it was fake nonetheless. "She is not our equal. She is a nobody. You don't need to slum it with that trash."

The flames snapped out at her, and this time it wasn't Sera's doing. The fire began to twist until a funnel of flames broke off from the barrier, skating toward her like an enraged tornado. Olivia planted her feet and refused to move. She glared at Kai through zigzag-cut bangs.

"You wouldn't dare."

Kai met her stare, his merciless eyes unblinking. A few seconds before the fire tornado would have collided into Olivia, she jumped aside.

"You son of a dragon's whore!" she screamed at him, raising her hands. Broken shards of brick rose into the air.

"Time to fight, boss?" Dal asked Kai as he and the other two commandos came up behind him.

The brick shards were humming softly. The countdown to their explosions into micro splinters had begun. This was going to hurt.

"There is no point in fighting," a voice echoed.

A gust of magic swept across the hollow husk of a room, putting out Kai's fire and grounding Olivia's bricks. Sera squinted her eyes, struggling to see past the smoke and shadows. A man stepped out of the darkness, flipping down his hood. It was Finn Drachenburg, and he was holding the Priming Bangles.

CHAPTER TWENTY-TWO

An Ancient Purpose

KAI STOOD VERY still, his eyes frozen over with cold fury. And those eyes stalked his cousin as he crossed the room. Finn took his place between Harrison and Olivia, handing each of them one pair of the Priming Bangles. Then he turned a smug smile on Kai.

"I thought you had people watching him," Sera whispered.

"I did."

"They decided to take a little nap," Finn told him, his smile growing wider.

"What do you think you're doing here, helping these miscreants?" the dragon demanded. His voice was low, his words oozing venom.

"Helping them?" A demented laugh burst from Finn's mouth. "No, no. You are mistaken. I'm not helping them." He stood taller. "I'm leading them."

Kai's face went blank, but his eyes were boiling over with volcanic vengeance. "Explain yourself."

"You're not in charge here, Kai. I am. In this room, I am king, and you are nothing. Your position is irrelevant.

Your magic is irrelevant. Except in how it can serve us." Finn smirked at him. "And you *will* be helping us."

Kai folded his arms across his chest. "No. I will not. Unlike all of you, my mind is not weak. I can fight the mind control you could not."

"You misunderstand. Everything."

"I'm still waiting for you to start making sense."

"I'm not controlling them," Finn said. "They're acting of their own free will."

"The madness in their eyes indicates otherwise."

"That is not madness. It is magic unfettered, broken from the bonds that have held us back for far too long."

Sera looked into his eyes. That spark—it was not magic intoxication like she'd thought; it was the spark of a fanatic. "You lied to us."

And her magic hadn't picked it up. Neither had Kai's. Finn was dabbling in some seriously strong magic.

Mock shock washed across the fanatic's face. "Did I? Oh, dear."

"There's no magic apocalypse coming, is there?"

"A revolution, yes. An apocalypse, no. I might have played up the death and destruction a bit." He shrugged. "But how else could I lure Kai out of his protective perch in that ugly office building?"

"You were in control of your own body that day I fought you at Magical Research Laboratories."

Finn dipped his chin. "And what a glorious fight it was. You shattered my wind barrier with a single touch. A Magic Breaker. It's a rare skill, and their magic tends to be too weak to break any spell of consequence. You broke a first tier spell." He stepped forward. "I've never seen anything like you before."

Kai moved between them, his eyes screaming murder.

The dragon was dangerously close to the surface. "Stay away from her."

"We'll chat later," Finn promised Sera, then turned his gaze to Kai. "You don't understand. You think we are the enemy. We're not. We're the solution the supernatural world has been craving. We want a better future. And soon all of the other supernaturals will realize they do too. This is all for the greater good."

"Save the speeches," Kai snapped at him. "You're not going to convert me to your cult."

Finn let out a long, melodramatic sigh, one he'd clearly been practicing for a long time to get just right. "I knew you wouldn't see things our way. You never were a visionary, Kai." His voice dropped, and he added darkly, "So I wasn't planning on recruiting you to the cause. But that doesn't mean you can't be useful."

He motioned the Sage siblings forward. Harrison and Olivia each set one pair of the Priming Bangles into Finn's hands.

"Don't make me laugh." Steam simmered off of Kai's breath. "Am I supposed to be afraid of a few children's toys?"

"Oh, but the bangles are so much more than that. They have an ancient history. An ancient purpose. And you will help them fulfill it."

A ring of fire blazed up, trapping them inside with Finn and his lunatic army. Kai's eyes panned across the barrier, the crackling flames reflecting in them. He lifted his hand. Snowflakes began to fall.

"I wouldn't," Finn warned. "I've instructed my mages to start killing your comrades if you interfere. Good as you are, Kai, there are a lot more of us than there are of you. And you can't block all of our magic. Stand down if you want those four to live."

Kai's eyes narrowed to angry slivers as he met his cousin's stare. But he lowered his hand. The snowflakes hissed, dissolving into steam.

"Good," said Finn. "As I was saying, the Priming Bangles have an ancient history. Our family has an ancient history too. And you're the first of us in generations with the power of the dragon. You're as close to pure, undiluted magic that I'm going to find."

He waved four of the mages forward. Kai watched them surround him. He didn't move, but the look in his eyes froze them in their tracks.

"He won't bite. Kai is actually a very simple person, driven by a few very simple instincts. One of the strongest of these is the instinct to protect." Finn clinked the bangles at him. "It must conflict horribly with the bloodlust. Dragons are such moody creatures."

Taunt strings of lightning slid up Kai's arms.

"See what I mean?" Finn told his captive audience of madmen. "Once you understand how his simple mind works, you can control him. He won't fight us. He knows his friends will die, and he couldn't stand the guilt of letting that happen *again*."

The lightning fizzled out, and Kai's arms dropped to his sides. The dragon—the powerhouse mage, the confident and cocky man—he looked totally and completely defeated.

Finn gave his shoulder a patronizing pat. "Vampires draw their power by drinking the blood of others. The Priming Bangles are like that for magic: a conduit. Our family has been using them to allow experienced mages to boost our novices' magic until they learned to draw on their own. A waste of the bangles' true power! With a bit of old, forgotten magic, I can use them to drain your power. I've tested them out, and they work."

Euphoria drenched Finn's magic, crazed and insatiable. It broke through the false facade he'd managed to build up around himself—the clueless and underpowered cousin that had fooled not only her but Kai too. Right now, his magic was strong. Not Kai strong, but definitely first tier. He'd mentioned testing the bangles. Maybe he'd played vampire and snacked on a few mages' magic before making his grand entrance. And now he wanted to use those magic-leaching bracelets on Kai.

"Why?" Sera's voice was thick with anger, so thick that she could hardly speak.

Finn's magic snapped out at her, looking for holes in her defenses. She knew this game. She'd been playing it since the day she was born. She made her wall go invisible and her magic blank.

"I don't feel any magic from you." He frowned. "And I can't feel you blocking me. How did you do that?"

She glared at him. So even after gorging on magic, he wasn't as strong as his cousin. Her trick had never worked on Kai. "You are a poser," she told Finn. "A fraud."

"Some are born with powerful magic. The rest of us have to earn it." He shrugged. "I figured you of all people would appreciate the plight of the disenfranchised. After all, don't you have to deal with the insufferable behavior of the magic dynasties every day?"

Sera decided not to mention that he and at least two key players in his revolution were members of those magic dynasties. It would have gone right over their heads. So she kept her comments to herself, but she did step in front of him when he tried to slap the bangles onto Kai's wrists.

"Find another power source for your revolution."

"It's not so simple," Finn said, and he almost looked sorry. But he wasn't. She knew his type. He'd only fooled himself into thinking he was sorry because that fit his image of what a leader had to be: a martyr who would give up anything, even his own family, for the greater good. "I need a lot of power to boost all these mages, and Kai is the purest source of magic. I can do it without the bangles and without Kai—I've done it before, as you can see here—but the results vary."

So that's how all those mages had gotten more powerful. They'd leeched magic. That also explained the possessed look in their eyes and why they occasionally seemed more lucid than other times. They'd be most batty right after a magic gorge, and once it started to wear off, their minds settled a bit. Settled, not were sane. Sera hated the Magic Council with the force of a thousand exploding suns, but Finn's magic-sucking free-for-all was a million times worse. Every single one of his mages was out of their mind.

"The bangles help channel the magic, especially from a powerful mage," Finn said. "If we tried to drain Kai's magic without them, we'd likely make the whole island explode. That's what happened with Aiden in New York, and that overload took a chunk out of the city. Kai is many times stronger than Aiden."

Kai had mentioned the incident involving another Drachenburg cousin in New York City. If Finn's failed experiments were responsible for that much destruction, she'd hate to be there when he actually succeeded. He was the sort of person who'd destroy the world if it furthered his agenda.

"Why are you so casual about killing your own family?" she demanded. "Is that your vision of the future: every supernatural for themselves, only the strong survive, and screw all the humans?"

Finn's sigh was exasperated—and just a touch offended. "I'm not going to kill Kai. I'm just going to drain him. Then the magic inside of him will refill, and I can do it again. And again." He turned his greedy eyes on Kai. "As many times as I want. Unlimited renewable magic."

Finn's mages had clamped onto Kai, holding him still as their leader popped open the Priming Bangles. Sera tried to ram them, but three more mages split off from the main group and tackled her to the floor. She kicked and hit at them—and when that didn't work, she dug her fingernails into them and zapped them with magic. But more and more mages kept coming. Behind her, the commandos were fighting the mages who had swarmed through the door.

Sera's lip was bleeding and her head spinning as she crawled her way out from beneath the pile of dozing mages. At least she thought they were unconscious. Foam was frothing out of the mouth of that last one. She hoped he wasn't dead. Not because he didn't deserve it. She just didn't want to be the instrument of his demise. There was a big difference between killing a monster and killing a person. She'd done it before and would likely have to do it again, but she didn't particularly like it.

She danced around dive-bombing bricks and fireballs on her way to Kai. He wore one pair of the bangles around his wrists. Finn wore the other, his mouth spitting out chants. His words pulsed with dark, sinister magic. The echoes of it stung her skin. She felt dirty. A hundred showers wouldn't be enough to wash the filth of that magic away. There was something very, very wrong about it.

"Yes. Yes. Perfect." Finn grinned, high on magic. His

bangles glowed brighter with every passing second.

And as his bangles grew brighter, Kai's dulled. Finn was draining his magic, and from the look on Kai's face, it hurt. A lot. His fists were clenched, his neck stiff.

Horrified, Sera watched them. She'd never seen anything like this before. The world held no shortage of horrors, but this was pure evil.

Kai began to roar out, the song of his torment beyond horrible. Beyond belief. Symbols drawn in magical light pulsed across his skin, smoke sizzling up from them. He looked like he was on fire.

Sera couldn't think. She could only act. Not stopping to second guess herself, she rushed forward and planted one hand on Finn's bangles, the other on Kai's. Pain and magic ripped through her hands, frying every nerve in them. The burning river of magic shot down her arms, and liquified pain flooded into her chest, dripping down her ribs. As it pushed into her legs, her knees collapsed. Finn tried to throw her off. She couldn't even stand, but she clenched her teeth and held on, trying to concentrate on disrupting the flow of magic. She had to stop it.

Finn kicked her, but next to the pain wracking her body, it hardly registered. She could smell her hands burning. The fact that she couldn't feel them was very bad news, but she tried not to think about that. She had to break the magic draining Kai. She pushed against the tidal wave, willing it to shatter.

It laughed in her face.

She couldn't see anything anymore. She could hardly hear. The tidal wave was drowning her, its salty waters burning her nose and suffocating her breath. She was slipping.

A soft growl, a shadow of its former self, buzzed in the

air. Something about it was familiar, but her head was too water-logged to remember what. The growl came again. It said her name. Kai? Sera tried to open her eyes—to find him—but she saw only blackness.

"Sera," Kai's voice whispered in her ear.

"I'm lost," she muttered, fear filling her. "I don't know what to do."

"Break the magic."

"How?"

"Like before. Reverse it. Flip it inside out."

"Will that really work? Will it shatter the spell?"

He didn't answer. He was gone. She was alone again, alone inside the tidal wave. And if she didn't break it, she would die inside here.

Sera stretched her tired, torn magic out once more. She hooked onto a piece of the evil magic. It took all her willpower not to let go the moment she made contact. Slippery, oily, icy, it tried to slither away. She held on tighter, wrapping her magic around it like a warm blanket. It squirmed and flopped like a fish caught on land. Encouraged by its fear, Sera flipped her magic inside out. The tidal waves stilled—then shattered. As millions of tiny crumbs dissolved into the air, she opened her eyes.

The first thing she saw was the light going out of the Priming Bangles. They clicked open and fell to the floor.

The second thing she saw was Finn push Kai over and then, enraged, turn eyes saturated with magic on her.

CHAPTER TWENTY-THREE
Fear

BLOOD DRIPPED FROM Sera's nose. She wiped it away with the back of her hand, then reached back to draw her sword. Her fingers refused to close around the hilt. In fact, she still couldn't feel her hands. Retracting them, she stared down at burnt and blistered palms. So much for fighting.

"That looks bad," Finn taunted. "Do you want me to have one of my mages take a look at it?"

"Your mages will keep their magic to themselves if they know what's good for them," Sera spat back. Her body had blocked out all feeling to her hands, but she didn't need to be a doctor to know they were completely trashed.

"You're not in any position to be making threats."

Dragon fire flashed behind his eyes. He'd leeched a lot of magic from Kai. This was going to be fun.

"How's this for a threat? First, I'm going to knock the stolen magic out of you. Then, I'm going to make short work of your minions."

"There are many of us and so few of you." His grin was pure rapture. "Give up now."

"Yeah, so you've got to know by now that that's just not

going to happen."

"You're being stubborn."

Twin pillars of fire blazed up behind Finn, casting him in demonic light. Beside him, illuminated strands of bright silver magic began to twist and turn together, slowly shaping into a dragon.

"That's bigger than your last one," Sera commented. *Maybe if I wrap my legs and arms around it, I can...push out my magic and shatter it?*

Even in her head, the idea sounded ridiculous. Finn was high on Kai's magic, a power both potent and resilient—so potent and resilient that it had allowed Kai to survive being shot at by a tank.

"Yes, it is." Finn's dragon continued to grow. At this rate, it would be fully formed in another one or two minutes max.

"Callum," Sera said. "You go for the spatting siblings. Dal and Tony, start working your way through the rest of these bozos. I'll deal with Finn."

When they didn't charge into battle, she looked back. They just stood there, their eyes wide as they stared at the forming dragon. They were tough guys, but right now they looked scared out of their wits. Kai was struggling to peel himself off the floor, and they didn't move a muscle. Fear had frozen them.

Finn laughed. "You are alone, Sera. And yet you're not scared. Why is that?"

Not scared? Of course she was scared. She was terrified. But when you'd spent two decades in constant fear for your life, you'd long since learned to deal with the fear. You didn't let it paralyze you.

"Nothing scary about you," she told him. "All show and no substance."

The dragon's tail swung at Sera. She ducked. It came again, and she jumped back. The tail smacked the floor hard, crumbling it into a crater of cracked and broken pieces.

"No substance, you say? How about that!"

"She's right," Kai's scratchy voice said as he stumbled to his feet beside her. Sera extended her arm, and he gripped onto her shoulder, using it to steady himself. "You are playing a game. You've only ever played games."

The fire pillars doubled in diameter, forcing Finn's army to scramble to avoid the angry flames.

"Playing with magic is very different than fighting with it." Kai took a heavy step forward.

"Wait." Sera swung her arm down in front of him like a gate. "You're in no condition to fight."

He looked pointedly at her blistered hands.

"The rest of me is fine," she said.

He gave her a hard look.

"Mostly fine." Her body was sore and her head was pounding with the thumps of a herd of stampeding horses, but she was still standing. "I'm in better shape than you. He just drained your magic dry."

Kai stepped around her. "Not completely dry."

"I'll gladly take the rest," Finn called out.

That did it. Kai charged forward, preparing to tackle his cousin. But Finn threw him back with a gust of wind that slammed him against the wall. Sera jumped over the dragon's tail. Blasts of icy energy flew at her, nearly kissing her cheek as she rolled. They shattered against the back wall, singing out like frozen chimes. Sera jumped up and ran at him.

Finn's fist crackled with lightning. He swung a punch at her, but even juiced up as he was right now, he wasn't a fighter. Sera slid aside and slammed her elbow into his ribcage. Roaring in pain, Finn stumbled away. A ring of red and gold energy burst out of the floor, sending a shock through Sera's body.

She must have blacked out for a second because the next thing she remembered was lying on the floor, watching Kai body-slam Finn into a brick wall. Blood and sweat were smeared across both cousins' faces. Kai was barely staying on his feet, but he kept fighting, powered solely by fury. Finn looked even worse. His head was bleeding, his steps dizzy, and his arm hung at an awkward angle.

The summoned dragon had faded out to the point that it was nothing more than a ghost; soon it would disappear completely. The commandos were finally fighting. Finn's army was falling. Olivia and a few others lay unconscious in the corner. Harrison was making a run for the exit.

Kai hit Finn one final time, and the leader of the magic revolution crumpled to the floor. Kai pulled out a pair of handcuffs—a special type designed to block out all magic. As he slapped them onto his cousin's wrists, Harrison and a few other mages made their exit. Kai's eyes slid across the room, falling on Sera. He trudged over to her, his boots thumping heavily against the cracked floor.

"Hi," she croaked, trying to pull herself up. Her body refused to cooperate.

"Hi." He crouched down and wrapped his arm around her waist, helping her up. He nearly fell over. "You look like shit."

"Thanks, so do you."

She managed to sit. Her butt felt like someone had hit it with a war hammer. She looked around the room. Most of the mages had fled. The commandos had managed to capture a few. They were slapping magic-blocking handcuffs on them.

"We won?" she asked.

"Yes." A spark of magic flashed in his tired eyes. "Too bad you slept through the whole thing."

"Not all of it. I was cheering you on from here while trying to convince my body to get up."

The humor washed from his face. "Let me see your hands, Sera."

She showed them to him. A few of the blisters had popped and were oozing blood and pus.

"There was an enormous amount of magic streaming through those bangles," he said.

"Enormous? Come now. There's no need to be modest. How about gargantuan?"

"You tried to disrupt the flow of magic," he continued. Apparently, he didn't find her weak attempt at humor very funny. "You didn't just try, you did it. And it almost killed you. You almost died for me."

"Ha, you'd like to think so, wouldn't you? Maybe I did it to save the city from a cult of crazy mages."

He winked at her.

"I did."

"If saving the city was all you wanted, you could have just hit Finn over the head while he was draining my magic."

"What's your point?"

"He wasn't in any condition to stop you," he said.

"Yeah, well, as we've been over at least a hundred times, I'm not the smartest person in the world. I just did the first thing that came into my head."

"Your head? Or your heart?"

"You flatter yourself."

He chuckled. "You can deny it all you want, but your

actions speak for themselves. At that moment, you weren't thinking about saving the city. You were thinking about saving me. Stop," he said as she opened her mouth to argue.

It was just as well. She wasn't even sure what she'd say.

"We'll discuss this later," he said.

"Like hell we will. There's nothing to discuss."

"You just keep telling yourself that, sweetheart." He hovered his hand over hers. "I have just enough magic left to heal your hands."

"You mean, you can do something other than wreck devastation?"

"Yes, now push in that pouting lip before I bite it."

Following orders wasn't Sera's strong suit, but then she couldn't be sure he wasn't serious. He looked down at her hands. Almost immediately, the blisters began to shrink and close. Sera felt a rush of pain, which was quickly swallowed by a warm and smooth flood of soothing energy. She watched the raw burns fade to pink, then disappear completely.

"Wow." She moved her fingers, then clenched her hands into fists. "Thanks." She caught him as he toppled. "Are you all right?"

"Healing you took more magic than I'd expected," he muttered softly. "I'm out of practice."

"If you can't walk back to the boat, I'll just swing you over my shoulder and carry you there."

"You're not strong enough."

"Sure I am. I bench press dragons all the time."

He snorted. Sera waved the commandos over. They hadn't made it two steps when a heavy thud shook the building.

"What's that?" she asked.

Callum peered out the window. "Oh, no."

"Tell me."

"The mages didn't retreat. They went to gather reinforcements."

Sera hurried to the window and looked outside. They were trapped at the top of a guard tower, and below an army of mages, fairies, and a slew of nasty creatures were swarming inside.

CHAPTER TWENTY-FOUR

The Burning Tower

CALLUM AND DAL set up a barricade at the door. There wasn't much in the room, but they molded what little they could find into a thick magical paste that they slathered across every hinge and gap. Tony waited behind them, his eyes closed, his hands pressed to the wall.

"How many?" Kai asked him.

"A dozen Wondrous Ones—mostly elves and a few fairies. About as many mages. A flock of ravens. Some dark ponies."

Dark ponies weren't dark, at least not on the outside. They were pink, purple, and a million other different shades of pastel. Each one of them looked like it had wandered straight off the set of My Little Pony. Except they weren't friendly or sweet. Inside, they were as dark as midnight, those nasty little creatures. And they kicked hard.

"We have the defensive advantage," Callum said.

Something thumped against the door, and the glowing barrier sizzled like a glob of fat hitting the frying pan.

"Somehow, I don't think that's going to deter them,"

said Dal. He raised his gun to the bars on the window and fired. A raven the size of a house cat dropped out of the sky. "They're coming from both sides."

The floor shook with the force of an earthquake.

"All three sides," he amended, then shot another giant diving raven.

The door thumped again. And again. And again. They were getting into a rhythm. Low and steady beneath that pounding percussion beat, the floor buzzed. As clouds rolled across the sky, a blast of lightning hit the tower. Bricks erupted from the outside walls and tumbled to the ground like falling tears.

"The vampires have arrived," Dal called out from the window.

"Common vampires?" Sera asked.

"Yes."

Good news.

"But their eyes are glowing red."

Not so good news. Glowing red eyes meant bloodlust. Someone—probably that dolt Harrison—had gotten those vampires worked up, then unleashed them onto the tower. On the bright side, they'd probably do as much damage to their allies as to their target. Unfortunately, they could do a hell of a lot of damage before they conked out. They'd tear the tower down brick by brick to get to their target. Sera's guess was that target was either Kai or her. Harrison wouldn't have had to look far to find a sample of their blood. The top room of the tower was practically painted with it.

"It would seem Finn's revolution goes beyond a few disgruntled mages," Sera told Kai.

"So it would seem," he agreed.

A gust of northern wind rocked the tower. Snowflakes

fluttered in through the window. They coalesced into a single ice block that attached itself to the ceiling.

"I'll take the vampires," Sera offered as the block cracked open and tiny snow flurries began to fall softly to the ground.

"They're at the back of the army."

"Not anymore."

A pale hand plunged through the window, grabbing Dal by the throat. The vampire thumped him against the wall, then tossed him aside. The beast began to claw and scrape at the bars, his ruby eyes locked onto Sera. So Harrison had teased the vampire with her blood after all. Oh goody.

"Where do you think you're going?!" Kai shouted out.

She kept on walking. When she got to the window, she slammed a brick against the vampire's hand. As it roared out in pain, she did the same to the other hand, and the vampire dropped. Unfortunately, there were five others waiting to take his place.

"You're insane." Kai grabbed her arm, pulling her away from the window. "They've fed on magic."

"What?"

"You can see it in their eyes. That's not just plain bloodlust. They're high on magic too."

"Is that even possible?"

"Yes," he said. "I've seen it before. It just isn't done very often because no sane person would feed magic to a blood-starved vampire. It makes them stronger and meaner."

"Hmm."

He moved in front of her, blocking her view of the window. "Long range attacks only on them. Don't get within grabbing range."

"I don't have any long range attacks. Unlike some

people, I can't shoot lightning bolts out of my fingers."

Kai didn't move. He looked so weak right now that she could have pushed right past him, but that wouldn't solve their problem.

"How's Dal?" he asked.

Tony looked up from Dal's body. "Unconscious."

Which meant he probably wouldn't be fighting, and someone would have to carry him out of here. Assuming they could get out. The barrier at the door wasn't looking good. The magic was mostly drained. Callum lifted his hands to refill it, when the snowflakes in the air exploded into a net of lightning rays. Sera spun and tackled Kai to the ground before it hit them. Tony and Callum weren't so lucky. They hung suspended for a moment, convulsing on the line of pink and purple lightning. Then the magic flickered out, and the two men tipped over and hit the floor.

The magic barrier was full of holes. The assailants at the door were shredding the wood to splinters. Vampiric arms tore at the bars on the window. Half of them were already gone.

"Kai?" she whispered.

His eyes were locked on their fallen comrades.

"They're not dead," she said.

"No." He shook himself. "But they will be if we don't do something."

"Use your magic."

"I haven't got enough left to do any significant damage." He looked at her. "You. You need to do it. Hit them with your magic."

"I...I don't know how to control it."

He took her hands, setting them on the floor. He placed his over hers. "As the name suggests, elemental magic is magic we draw from the elements. Feel the stones of the tower. Feel the layers, stacking down one after the other, all the way to the ground. The earth. That's your tether."

A bar was ripped from the window. Sera jerked her head toward it.

"Close your eyes," Kai said.

"But the vampires…" She had the overwhelming urge to snatch up her sword and run at them.

"Forget the vampires. Close your eyes."

She let her eyelids drop.

"Now reach for the earth. Seek out its magic. Hear its song. Let everything else fall away."

Sera found it: a song of strength and resilience, of power and the everlasting. It was an ancient song, one the earth had been singing since long before any of them had been born.

"Good. Now hold onto it, let its power tether you," he whispered against her ear. "Know that with it as your ally, you are not alone. Open your eyes, Sera."

She did—and gasped when she saw the floor shaking softly beneath her. "What should I do? Split the ground out from under them?"

"Only if you want to bring down the whole tower and us along with it."

"Not really."

"The earth is the element that's easiest to use as a tether. It's constant," he said. "But all the elements are connected. You can reach them through the earth. Give it a try. Reach for fire."

She slid her magic along the channels of earth and listened for fire. It cracked and snapped in the distance, fast and fleeting. It sang out to her, daring her to give chase.

But she didn't. Instead, she tugged on one of the notes that formed its song, drawing it to her. Magic shot across the strand and up her arms. It didn't hurt. It sizzled lightly against her skin, tickling her fingertips.

She pushed the flames up, higher and higher. The adrenaline rush was unbelievable. A shrill scream called out. She opened her eyes to watch a vampire bathed in fire fall off the window. She dug her nails into the cracked floor, reaching deeper for more magic. But she wasn't just reaching deep into the ground; she was reaching deep inside herself, pulling out her magic. And that magic came tumbling out like a hundred chiffon scarfs all tied together. The more she pulled, the more of her magic spilled out. It was bursting from her fingertips.

Flames licked the walls and slid across the ceiling, swallowing the block of ice. Steam filled the room. She bathed in the wet, hot air.

"Sera."

She grinned at Kai. His hair was sticking up at a dozen different angles. "You look funny."

"The fire."

"Disorderly."

"You need to stop it."

She giggled. "If you could only see yourself, you'd flip out at the messiness of it."

He pinched her hands.

"Ouch!"

"You're drunk on magic."

"Nope."

"You need to rein it in, or you'll kill us all."

She stared into his eyes. They were just so...serious. She exploded into laughter.

"Ok, let's try this a different way." He coughed. "Reach

for water. Use it to put out the fire."

"Why would I do a silly thing like that? I like fire. I like making things burn."

"Burning things is fun." He leaned into her, his words feather-light against her cheek. "But it's nothing compared to the high you get when exploding that fire into steam." He slid his hand down her arm. "Fire is intense. It burns out, and then it is gone. Water lingers. It's smooth and soft, seducing you with its touch until you can't even remember fire's name."

"Ok." Sera blew him a kiss. "I'll give this water fellow a try."

She scraped her hands across the floor, searching it out. She found something else entirely.

"Oh, hello, you," she purred, tugging on the magic. It wasn't as old as an element, but it was far more exotic.

"What is it?"

"Glyphs. They're going stale, though."

"I don't see them."

"Of course not. They're hidden," she told him.

"Can you reveal them?"

"Sure. Why not?"

She peeled away the invisible cloak, and the concealed glyphs pulsed to life beneath them before fading.

"They are not lit up," said Kai.

"You need to pour your magic into the glyphs." Her head was clearing, at least enough to realize that the air was drenched in smoke. "That's how you activate them." Sweat slid down her face. She coughed. "This air is awful."

"Welcome back."

She threw his hands off of hers. "I didn't go anywhere."

"No?" Kai winked at her. "How about we all get out of here?"

"Sounds splendid."

He jumped up. He dragged Callum to the glyphs, then Tony. He was going back for Dal when a glowing ball of silver magic shot through the flames protecting the door and hit him square in the chest. He lost his hold on Dal, and they both tumbled down.

Burst after of burst of silver light shot out of the flames, like someone had found a way to stuff magic balls into a futuristic ray gun. The swarm of them whooshed overhead and hit the wall, splattering like bugs against a windshield. Keeping low, Sera grabbed a hold of Kai and Dal and dragged them onto the glyphs.

"Hey." She climbed over Kai to look him in the face. "Are you awake?"

He cracked open a single eye. "Barely."

"I need your help. You've got to activate the glyphs, so we can get out of here."

"Can't," he muttered. "I'm dry."

"What do you mean, you're dry?"

"No magic left. I need to recharge."

"How long?" she asked him.

"Longer than we have."

Past the flames, angry voices were screaming curses and spells. Large chunks of the walls exploded, raining down broken shards and burning ashes on everyone in the room. A vampire was squeezing through the window. Behind the beast, at least three more were waiting. All were hungry. The roof shook with heavy tremors.

They'd run out of time.

Sera looked down at Kai. His messy hair didn't seem so funny anymore. His collapse was the writing on the wall, the message that the last defense had fallen. Even the dragon could no longer fight. She was all they had left—she and her abominable magic. If only she knew what she was doing.

Mages, fairies, vampires, beasts… They flooded into the room, their eyes promising death. Death, not pain. They were the cleanup crew, Sera realized. They were going to make sure none of them lived to speak of what had happened here.

"Stop!" Sera shouted out, surprised when they actually did. But it was only a matter of time before they realized that she did not command them.

She wasn't going to wait for that time to come. She slapped her hands down hard on the floor, pouring her magic into the glyphs. She drew out everything she had, everything she'd spent years burying. It flooded her, burning through her veins. It gushed into the glyphs, and they swallowed it all up greedily, bursting to life with a sapphire glow. The lines spread across the floor, the blinding blue light swallowing the room whole.

Sera's stomach lurched, then she landed with a thud, sliding against an icy marble floor. Tony was there beside her, and Callum and Dal and even Finn too. But where was Kai? She pulled herself across the floor by her hands, scouring the room for him.

She found him under the desk, his eyes closed. She tapped his cheek to wake him.

He caught her hand. "Sera." His eyes opened. "This looks like my office."

"Yes."

"The others?"

"All here. And Finn too."

"And the enemy?"

"Except for Finn, they're all back in that burning, crumbling tower as far as I know."

"Good." He pressed his lips to her fingertips. "Now, help me up, please. We're going to have that talk."

CHAPTER TWENTY-FIVE

Magic Ignited

DESPITE THE DRAGON'S threat, they didn't have a talk about Sera's magic that day. Not ten seconds after she'd pulled him out from under his desk, a horde of Drachenburg employees swarmed into the office. Their arrival had apparently triggered a silent alarm. As Kai went through the play-by-play with a room full of his overwrought advisors, Sera slipped out. The look he gave her as she left stated clearly enough that this wasn't over. Maybe not, but she needed a long shower and a good night's sleep before going toe to toe with the dragon again.

Nearly half a week went by without any word from him. Sera was just beginning to hope that she'd never hear from him again, when she got called into Simmons's office. He was sending her to Drachenburg Industries for a 'closing meeting'. Whatever that meant. Probably something Kai had insisted on so that he could force her into this 'talk' he wanted to have. And he went through Simmons so she couldn't say no. Bastard.

This time when Sera entered the building, there was someone waiting for her. A taciturn man in a sleek black suit escorted her up to Kai's office, then left her alone with the dragon in the room.

Kai rose from his desk, as always dressed in dark jeans and a fitted black t-shirt. God, he looked good. Sera clenched her fists behind her back and stepped forward.

"Sera," he said, magic pulsing beneath each syllable. The few days of rest had recharged him. He was as powerful as ever. And as deadly, she reminded herself.

"Mr. Drachenburg."

The corner of his mouth kicked up in a half-smile. "I thought we were past that." He circled around his desk and set his hands on her shoulders.

She shrugged him off. "I'm here on official guild business, not to cuddle up to the dragon."

"Very well then." He leaned his hands back against the desk. "Harrison and Olivia got away. The Magic Council has sentenced Finn to imprisonment at Atlantis."

That was their code name for a supernatural prison in the middle of the Atlantic Ocean. Only a select few knew where it was, and Sera wasn't one of them. It was just as well. The fewer people there were who knew where to find him, the better off everyone was. Finn had accumulated quite a following. The last thing anyone needed was for them to spring him out of prison.

"Did he happen to mention how his minions got past your security?"

"Yes. He joined them every time. He broke through the security." The reluctant words scraped out of his mouth.

"You said no one with selfish or nefarious reasons could get in." And Finn's intentions had been dripping with both.

"He claimed he was acting in the best interests of the supernatural community," Kai said, frowning. "I think he actually believes it."

Well, Finn *was* nuts.

"And the guys? Are they all right?" she asked.

"Tony, Dal, and Callum have fully recovered. I've awarded them each a bonus and the rest of the month off."

"They deserve it after what they went through."

"Yes."

"And the Priming Bangles?" she asked.

"Safe. They are somewhere no one will find them."

"Good."

"I've sent Mayhem the payment."

"I figured as much when Simmons didn't send me here to take it out of you with my sword."

"How much of that payment will you get?"

"Not much," she said. "But more than I usually get."

"You saved me from that torment." He rubbed his hand across his wrist, as though he could still feel the bangle there. "You could have left, but you didn't. You risked your life to save me. You nearly drowned the tower in magic. And then you activated the glyphs and got us all out of there."

"It was no big deal."

"No big deal?" he said. "You told me the range of transport is dependent on the magic level of the person activating the glyphs. You transported us over the water and across town. I'm not even sure I could have brought us so far."

"What's your point?"

"My point," he said, pushing off his desk. "...is your magic is off the charts. If you told Simmons about it, he'd have to pay you more."

Only after the Magic Council had tested her. No thank you. "We've been through this before."

He sighed. "If you're going to insist on keeping your

magic a secret, you should at least let me train you to control it so you don't end up getting someone killed."

"I can control it."

He arched a dark eyebrow at her.

"I'll work on it," she promised. "Ok?"

"Ok, I'll be keeping track of your progress," he said, his eyes shimmering like blue glass. "As long as you keep your magic under control and don't go off on mad, drunken rages through the city, it can just be our little secret."

"Even from the Council?"

He watched her for a few seconds that seemed to stretch onto eternity. "Yes," he finally said. "They don't need to know. If they found out, they'd get you tied up in all these tests, which would interfere with my plan."

"And what is your plan?"

"Oh, no. You'll just have to wait and see."

"I hope it doesn't involve wrapping me up in bacon and feeding me to the dragon for dinner."

"Well, you are tasty…"

"Kai!"

He chuckled.

"If that's all you needed, I'll just be go—"

He caught her hand as she turned to leave. "Not so fast. I'm not done."

"Oh?"

"Try not to look so scared."

"I'm not scared of you." Sera tried to slip out of his hold, but he had the grip of a tyrannosaurus rex. She growled at him. "What do you want?"

"Any one of the supernaturals we faced was powerful enough to make most people turn and run. You stood your ground against an army of them. And Mayhem will give you, what, twenty percent of what I paid them?"

"Fifteen."

He frowned. "You deserve something extra."

"Maybe. But this is what I get. I knew what I was getting into when I signed on with them."

"I want to give you something extra."

"No."

"Why not?"

"Firstly," she said. "Because it's against the conditions of my contract with Mayhem. And secondly, because I don't want your money."

"You need it." He pointed at her feet. "Your shoes are falling apart. Your clothes are torn. And you should eat decently once in a while."

"Since when is pizza not decent food?"

He brushed her pitiful joke aside. "If you won't take the money, at least let me take you to dinner."

In her head, Naomi's voice screamed out, *Date! Date! Date!*

"I don't think that would be a very good idea," Sera told him.

"It's a spectacular idea." He leaned in closer, his magic electrifying the air around them. It purred against her skin. "You're attracted to me."

She shook her head.

He grinned. "You are. I can see it in the way your body moves toward mine."

She tried to step away, but his hand settled on her lower back, holding her in place. "I'm not moving toward you. You're holding me prisoner."

"Should I let go?"

No. "Yes."

As he dropped his hands, he leaned in to whisper into her ear, "I'm waiting."

"For what?" she asked, her breath catching in her throat. His words were like honey against her skin.

"For you to prove me wrong and run off." He kissed her neck once, so softly that she wondered if she'd only imagined it.

"I..."

"I don't think you will." He met her gaze. "Even now, you're thinking about kissing me. You're wondering if it's as good as you remember. It is."

"You're delusional."

"Am I? Did I only imagine the need pulsing through your magic as you kissed me back?"

"Kissed you back? Please. I was trying to push your tongue away." Even as she said the words, she knew it was a weak lie.

"Oh?"

He stroked his hand down her face, his eyes burning into her. When she looked into those eyes, she knew how bone-shattering amazing it would be to be with him—if only she could tame him. But deep down, she knew he could never be tamed. And she liked it. That was the truth of it. She was drawn to the wild and deadly dragon. She wanted him to bathe her body in fire.

"You can still walk away," he said. His lips brushed against hers.

"I really should," she agreed, leaning into him as her mouth trailed his.

The moment he kissed her, their magic ignited. He was right. Kissing him was every bit as good as she remembered. Magic sizzled from his fingertips as his hands slid down her body, following her every curve. It had been so long—too long—since anyone had touched her like this. No, screw that. *No one* had ever touched her quite like this.

She'd never been caressed by magic. She'd always stayed away from supernaturals. It had been too risky. Being with one of them meant risking exposure. It made her vulnerable.

And right now she just didn't care. In fact, Kai could expose her like this all day long as far as she was concerned. His teeth nipped lightly at her neck.

The door to the office whooshed open. Sera scrambled off the desk—how had she gotten there?—and watched Kai's secretary walk across the room. Kai's shirt was tossed over the back of his chair, and half of Sera's hair was falling out of her ponytail. The woman didn't even blink. She set a stack of papers down on Kai's desk, right beside where he was sitting. She reminded him about a press conference later that day, then clicked her runway heels back across the room and closed the door.

As soon as she was gone, Kai turned his brilliant blue eyes on Sera. They shone with a foreboding light, one that promised pain and pleasure. He wasn't the least bit mortified that they'd been interrupted while making out on his desk. Realization, that heavy stone of no denial, sank in Sera's stomach. His secretary hadn't looked shocked because he did this sort of thing all the time.

But she didn't do things like this. Not ever. All those reasons why she hadn't been with a man in so long—they were valid here too. They were even more valid actually. Kai was on the Magic Council, the organization that had made being Dragon Born a death sentence. Sera couldn't risk her life—the lives of her family—for a man who was just playing games with her because he got his thrills off of seducing women who'd turned him down. That wasn't the recipe for a healthy relationship. She didn't know anything about relationships, but even she knew that.

"Sera," he said, taking a step toward her.

She backed away. "Yeah, so I'm going now."

He swung around, blocking her way. "We need to talk about this."

"No, we really don't."

"Or we could just pick up where we left off."

She blocked his hand, pushing it away. "I'm not letting you near me again. Not ever."

"Why not?" he asked. The look in his eyes was pure sin.

So she focused on the air over his shoulder instead. "You make me lose all sense of reality."

She realized her mistake as soon as she said the words, and his satisfied smile only reaffirmed that.

"That's a good thing," he said.

"No, it's not." She stood as tall as she could and put on her best official-sounding voice as she quoted the lines from the guild's procedure handbook, "Our business is concluded now. Mayhem thanks Drachenburg Industries for your prompt payment."

"Very impressive, Sera," he said. "Did you have to practice long to sound so stiff and pompous?"

She'd memorized the lines years ago. She'd just never used them before. Because he was right. They really were stiff and pompous. She preferred to wing it, but winging it with Kai had gotten her into nothing but trouble.

"Mr. Simmons values your business. If there is anything Mayhem can do to assist you in the future, please don't hesitate to contact him directly," she finished, passing him.

"Oh, our business is far from over," he said, his words following her out the door. "I'll be in touch all right."

And he wasn't referring to Mayhem.

CHAPTER TWENTY-SIX

The Bearer of Magic News

A FEW DAYS later, Sera came home from work exhausted. She'd fought more than a few horrible monsters that day. It had been nasty and gory—and so completely normal. Routine even. Routine was good. It meant monsters and goo and all kinds of disgusting gunk. There was no drama, no crazy mage cults trying to take over the world, and absolutely positively no big-headed mage shifters who turned into dragons.

Most of all, routine meant a nice, quiet Friday pizza night at home, where the only villains present were confined to the television screen. Riley had promised to order two large pizzas with extra cheese. This was definitely an extra cheese sort of day. Chasing a flock of crotchety harpies across the city was exhausting work, especially when they could fly and Sera was stuck on foot. After that ordeal, she was hungry enough to finish one of those pizzas all by herself.

She could hear the television playing when she came through the front door. The hot, cheesy aroma of pizza wafted down the hall, a delicious beacon drawing her onward to the living room. Halfway there, hunger gave way to dread.

He was here. His magic hummed through the living room like a well-tuned orchestra in an acoustic hall, the vibrations buzzing and bouncing off her skin. The heavy, potent—and yet sweet—scent of dragon magic drowned out the pizza. She was almost as mad about that as his intrusion. Ruining pizza night was a criminal offense as far as Sera was concerned, and he'd managed to do it two weeks in a row.

Riley turned his head, looking at her over the back of the sofa. "Hey, Sera."

Two open pizza boxes lay atop the coffee table, only a handful of slices left inside of each. An old horror movie cheesier than the pizza played on the television. Kai lifted a slice from the box, then threw back a wink at Sera.

"What the hell is he doing here?" she demanded.

"Joining us for pizza night," said Riley.

"Like hell he is."

"Now you're just being rude. You already tried to kick him out the last time he visited. Kai might start to think you don't like him."

"No worries," he told Riley. "I know she adores me."

Sera's jaw locked up. She started counting down from ten. *Ten, nine.* "Your 'friend'—and I hesitate to even call him that—"

"With or without the implied quote marks," said Kai.

Riley snorted.

Eight, seven, six. "—has been lying to you from day one. He lied to you about what he is, who he is—"

Riley turned to Kai. "Wait, so you aren't really a first tier mage who shifts into a dragon and heads the San Francisco branch of Drachenburg Industries?"

Sera gaped at them in disbelief.

"He told me everything."

Five. Four. "Oh, how grand of you." She shot Kai her best saccharine smile. "At what point did you finally admit to my brother that you've only been pretending to be his friend?" *Three! Two! ONE!* "And that you have been lying and manipulating him all in some demented attempt to spy on me because you are—wait, what's that? Oh, right. A freaking psychopath!"

"Are you a psychopath?" Riley asked Kai.

Kai shrugged. "Only some of the time."

She growled at them.

"Careful, sweetheart." Magic burned behind his eyes. "Some might take that as an invitation."

"You're hitting on me here? Really? In front of my own brother?"

He turned to Riley. "Do you mind?"

"No. In fact, please do. Take her out. Show her some fun. Someone has to. She's so tense that you could bounce lightning off of her head."

One of the pizza boxes burst into flames.

"I see what you mean." Kai waved his hand, and the flames dissolved into steam. The box was slightly charred around the edges but otherwise undamaged. The air now stank of dragon magic and fire, though. Kai gave her a stern look. "What happened to controlling your magic?"

"You invaded my home."

"I see. I make you lose all sense of reality. Isn't that what you said?"

She glared at him and imagined his hair on fire.

"If she actually said that to you, she must really like you," Riley told him. "Sera doesn't get emotional over just anyone. Though there was that one guy...Zachary, wasn't it?"

"I didn't get emotional over him. I planted magic bamboo on his front lawn."

Magic bamboo was just like normal bamboo—except it grew a few thousand times faster.

"She did it in the middle of the night," said Riley. "By morning, his lawn was so overgrown with the stuff that he couldn't open his front door. He had to climb out of a second story window to escape."

"Magic bamboo is a heavily controlled magical species. You need a special license to buy it. How did you get your hands on something like that?" Kai asked her.

Sera held up her hand before Riley could answer. "Don't tell him. If he knew, he'd feel obligated to report it to his colleagues on the Magic Council."

"I haven't told them about your magic," said Kai.

"Yet. I'm still waiting for the other shoe to drop," Sera replied.

"I don't drop shoes," he told her. "I throw them."

"Of that I have no doubt. You probably set them on fire first too."

"Naturally." He smirked at her. "I like making things burn."

The words smacked against her—her own words, ones she'd spoken while drunk on magic back in the burning tower. It was a reminder that she'd come too far. She'd allowed her magic out, and now she was having a hard time pushing it back down again. And no matter what she said, it wasn't just because of Kai. He rubbed away at her control more than anyone else, but even when he wasn't around, it was a constant struggle to keep her magic in check. It had taken on a life of its own, a wild and glorious and devastating life.

Maybe that's why the Dragon Born had all been killed. Maybe they really did become monsters. But she couldn't exactly go digging for answers because that would mean admitting what she was—and facing punishment.

"Tell me about this Zachary. Did you sleep with him?" Kai's tone was almost clinical, as though he were asking her to describe a foot fungus.

"First of all, that's none of your business," she said. "And second of all, yuck!"

"Good."

"He used to work for Mayhem too. One day, he decided it was his mission in life to annoy Sera. Out of the blue, of course." Riley grabbed a pizza slice from the box. "Or so Sera claims."

She watched a glob of hot cheese dangle precariously off the tip. "Are you going to eat that?" she asked Riley.

"Yeah, but there's more. If you sit down with us, we'll even share it with you."

Sera looked pointedly at Kai.

"You're not kicking him out. He's my friend, and he saved your life." Riley nodded. "That's right. He told me everything about your grand adventure fighting a cult of insane mages."

Sera hoped Kai hadn't told him *everything*. Her brother really didn't need to know that she and Kai had made out on top of his desk. Sera didn't even need to know that. Or remember it. Or whatever.

"Actually," Kai said, his eyes twinkling with mischief. "Sera and I saved each other."

"Fine," she sighed. "I'll just go to bed then."

"Are you sure? We saved a whole pizza just for you," Kai said.

She stopped mid-stride and pivoted around. "Show

me."

He held up a box from Wizard House Pizza, and her hunger returned with a vengeance. She felt her feet walking toward it. The promise of pizza had a special magic of its own, a magic aided by a long and exhausting day spent chasing harpies. Hunger battled it out with her resolution not to go anywhere near that man.

Hunger won.

Sera plopped down on the sofa between Riley and Kai, knowing she'd regret this. Just not as much as she'd regret it with an empty stomach. The dragon handed over the pizza box.

"It's still warm," she said in surprise.

"He magicked it," Riley told her. "Some sort of slow-burn fire spell."

She looked at Kai. "You magicked my pizza to stay warm?"

"Is that a problem?"

"Only if you changed the taste."

"It should taste the same."

"No problem then." She gave the pizza box a loving pat.

Riley snickered. "Careful, Kai. She might decide you're worth keeping around after all."

"Hmm."

Sera was about to open the box, when the doorbell rang. She looked at the door and sighed.

"I'll get it," Riley offered.

"No, I'll do it." With her luck, it was vampires. Or harpies. She passed him the box. "Just keep your paws off my pizza while I'm gone."

Sera walked down the hall, the pleasant scent of dough and cheese calling out to her, begging her to return.

Whoever had interrupted her date with the pizza had better already be dead—or they soon would be.

She opened the door to find a man in a smart suit standing outside. He didn't smell dead, but his magic had a potent pinecone-like smell. It was obvious even under the thick layer of spicy aftershave he wore. A mage. Oh, goody.

"Serafina Dering?"

"I am."

"My name is James Holloway," he said, handing her a large black envelope.

Sera turned it over in her hands. Her heart nearly stopped when she saw the crimson wax seal of the Magic Council on the back.

"It has come to the Council's attention that you are an unregistered mage. According to Article 3, Section 15 of the Supernatural Decree of 1993, all combative mages with a power level of Tier Five—also known as 'Standard'—or above are required to register with the Magic Council. You have recently demonstrated combative magic at or above that level. We have created a preliminary profile for you in our system until which time your abilities can be properly tested."

"Tested?"

"At the next Magic Games, which are scheduled to take place next month. You have been added to the register." He indicated the envelope. "All the information is in there, including your testing schedule and the rules of the Games. If you have any questions about your obligations, please call the number listed on the contact page. I wish you a pleasant evening and best of luck in the Games."

With that said, he dipped his chin to her and turned to walk away. Sera closed the door, her hands numb. Her whole body was numb—numb and hot. Her pulse pounded against her skin, burning it with fear. In a daze, she staggered back to the living room. The moment he saw her, Kai jumped up and hurried over.

"What happened? You look like someone died."

"No, no one's dead." Not yet anyway. With the Magic Council on to her, though, it was only a matter of time.

"Your magic is…unsettled. It's crashing too fast. You need to eat now."

"I'm not hungry."

"That's ok." He set his arm across her back, leading her to the sofa. "You can just watch me eat then."

She tried to laugh, but it came out as more of a grunt.

"What's wrong?" Riley asked her as she collapsed onto the sofa beside him.

Kai sat down on her other side, and she handed her brother the envelope. His eyes panned across the black paper, growing wide when he saw the bumpy crimson seal.

"The Magic Council?" he asked in a soft whisper.

"Their messenger informed me that I've been entered into the next Magic Games."

"The Magic Games are dangerous."

"Not any more dangerous than the things I've faced before. If I meet something nasty, I'll just bash it with my sword as always," she told him with a forced smile. Not that she believed a word of it. But there was no point in worrying Riley.

Kai held out his hand. "Let me see that."

"Sure. Why not?" she said with a laugh and handed it over. He probably knew everything inside it anyway. Maybe he'd even stamped the letter himself. He might as well have stamped her death sentence. She'd been such a fool.

Paper cracked and split as Kai tore open the envelope. He pulled out a slim folder with an embossed logo: the four symbols of the Mage Triad, the Vampire Covenant, the League of Fairies, and the Circle of the Otherworldly arranged in a ring. Then he began to flip through the papers inside.

"How did they find out?" Riley asked her.

"I wonder."

"I can feel your burning glare trained on me," Kai said, his eyes still scanning through the papers. "But this wasn't my doing. I promised I wouldn't tell them about your magic, and I didn't. I haven't even met with the Council since we started working together. Too busy fighting crazy mages and all that. And then I was recovering from fighting crazy mages. The Council sent me a message about Finn's sentence... Finn." He looked up at her. "Finn must have said something about you while being questioned."

"Questioned? I hope that's not a euphemism for tortured."

"Finn wasn't brought in for stealing cookies, Sera. He tried to spearhead a revolution."

"Even so, torture is wrong."

"It's how it's sometimes done. You would know that if you'd embraced your magic and integrated into our community rather than hiding from it."

"Oh, so this is my fault now?"

"No, it's not your fault. It's just how it is," he said. "Don't be so squeamish."

"That's easy for you to say. You step on people!"

"One person. And he was a werewolf about to kill you."

"Who do I look like—Little Bo Peep? I have a sword and I know how to use it, dragon breath."

"Dragon breath?"

"You heard me."

"Hearing and believing are two entirely different things,

sweetheart. I thought you knew better than to antagonize someone who steps on people."

"Ha! So you admit it!"

He licked his lips.

"What's in the letter?" Riley said quickly.

Kai gave Sera a look that could have burned the needles off a giant talking cactus, then turned to Riley. "It's just the standard package of forms. It says the Magic Games will be used to test her abilities and gauge her power level for her entry into the registry. Most mages are motivated to show off their magic because the better they rank in the Games, the more opportunities open up to them. Though I have a feeling Sera is going to be obstinate."

"I'll bust the monsters with my sword," she said. "No magic required."

"You're very good," Kai told her. "But that won't be enough. The Magic Games are dangerous. They're meant to push you to the extent of your magic, so the judges can get a good idea of your abilities. Swords won't be enough. And in most matches, they're not even allowed. Look here." He pointed at the page with her fight schedule. "They're starting you out in the Tier Three Division, which means they're pretty sure your magic is at least Substantial. My guess is they expect you to fight your way up the divisions from there."

"Couldn't Sera just pretend not to have magic?" Riley asked.

"No. The Magic Games are over two thousand years old. That's two thousand years we've had to figure out exactly how to get into a mage's head," Kai said. "The current Game Architect is very good. He's been running the Magic Games for over ten years and not once has he failed. He will throw every weapon in his extensive and exceptionally well-funded arsenal at you until he cracks open your magic. The stress of it…"

"You broke?" Sera asked in surprise.

"The stronger the mage, the harder he breaks. Of course I broke. We all broke. But then we pulled ourselves back together and were stronger for it. It helped that I had a coach to prepare me before the Games. Some of the mages didn't even have that."

"Everyone who wasn't born into the wealth of one of the prestigious dynasties, you mean," she said.

"Yes."

Riley gave her shoulder a squeeze.

"I'll be fine," she reassured him—and herself.

"Yes, you will be," said Kai. "Because I'm going to coach you."

Riley's hand dropped off her shoulder, and they both stared at him.

"Don't you have better things to do than save my bacon?" she stammered.

"Shh, don't try to talk him out of helping you," Riley whispered.

"I don't want his help."

"But you *do* need it."

She slouched down, drowning in the collapse of her own denial. "I know."

"Is that a yes?" Kai asked her.

"Yes."

"Ok, then we'll start tomorrow. The next Magic Games start in twenty-four days' time. I'll have only weeks to teach you magic other mages have had years to master. It won't be easy. Or painless."

"I understand. And I'm ready."

"No, you're not," he told her. "But you're strong. You'll

be all right."

Sera rose into her knees and leaned in to kiss him on the cheek. "Thank you," she whispered into his ear.

"I'll expect a favor in return," he whispered back.

"Such as?"

He pulled back, giving her a wide grin. "Oh, I'm sure I'll think of something."

Author's Note

If you want to be notified when I have a new release, head on over to my website to sign up for my mailing list at http://www.ellasummers.com/newsletter. Your e-mail address will never be shared, and you can unsubscribe at any time.

If you enjoyed *Mercenary Magic*, I'd really appreciate if you could spread the word. One of the best ways of doing that is by leaving a review wherever you purchased this book. Thank you for your invaluable support!

What's coming next in the series?

Magic Edge, the first book of *Dragon Born Alexandria*, is coming in November 2015. It follows the adventures of Sera's sister Alex. *Magic Games*, the second book of *Dragon Born Serafina*, will also be coming soon.

About the Author

Ella Summers has been writing stories for as long as she could read; she's been coming up with tall tales even longer than that. One of her early year masterpieces was a story about a pigtailed princess and her dragon sidekick. Nowadays, she still writes fantasy. She likes books with lots of action, adventure, and romance. When she is not busy writing or spending time with her two young children, she makes the world safe by fighting robots.

Originally from the U.S., Ella currently resides in Switzerland. She is the author of the epic fantasy series *Sorcery and Science* and the urban fantasy series *Dragon Born*.

www.ellasummers.com

Made in the USA
San Bernardino, CA
08 February 2016